W9-AXO-252

"It's heaven," Charity sighed

They paused to look around the wintry Norwegian countryside, and then the professor bent his head to kiss her.

"Don't do that," Charity said severely, willing her heart to regain its steady beat.

The professor looked down at her. "Another word for Charity is love. Shall I call you that?"

"Certainly not." Charity's heart ached. Everything was getting out of hand. "Please don't talk like that—do remember Brenda. I'm sure you miss her."

He was still looking at her, his mouth curved in a tender smile. "I fancy that we have our wires crossed," he observed calmly and then he kissed her again, very gently. "I do not like to be thwarted," he said finally.

Betty Neels is well-known for her romances set in the Netherlands, which is hardly surprising. She married a Dutchman and spent the first twelve years of their marriage living in Holland and working as a nurse. Today she and her husband make their home in a small ancient stone cottage in England's West Country, but they have returned to Holland often. She loves to explore tiny villages and tour privately owned homes there, in order to lend an air of authenticity to the background of her books.

Books by Betty Neels

These books may be available at your local bookseller.

Don't miss any of our special offers. Write to us at the following address for information on our newest releases.

Harlequin Reader Service
901 Fuhrmann Blvd., P.O. Box 1397, Buffalo, NY 14240
Canadian address: P.O. Box 603,
Fort Erie, Ont. L2A 9Z9

Two Weeks to Remember

Betty Neels

Harlequin Books

TORONTO • NEW YORK • LONDON
AMSTERDAM • PARIS • SYDNEY • HAMBURG
STOCKHOLM • ATHENS • TOKYO • MILAN

Original hardcover edition published in 1986
by Mills & Boon Limited

ISBN 0-373-02808-3

Harlequin Romance first edition December 1986
Second printing January 1987.

Copyright © 1986 by Betty Neels.
Philippine copyright 1986. Australian copyright 1986.
All rights reserved. Except for use in any review, the reproduction or utilization
of this work in whole or in part in any form by any electronic, mechanical
or other means, now known or hereafter invented, including xerography,
photocopying and recording, or in any information storage or retrieval system,
is forbidden without the permission of the publisher, Harlequin Enterprises
Limited, 225 Duncan Mill Road, Don Mills, Ontario, Canada M3B 3K9. All the
characters in this book have no existence outside the imagination of the
author and have no relation whatsoever to anyone bearing the same name
or names. They are not even distantly inspired by any individual known
or unknown to the author, and all incidents are pure invention.

The Harlequin trademarks, consisting of the words HARLEQUIN ROMANCE
and the portrayal of a Harlequin, are trademarks of Harlequin Enterprises
Limited; the portrayal of a Harlequin is registered in the United States Patent
and Trademark Office and in the Canada Trade Marks Office.

Printed in U.S.A.

CHAPTER ONE

CHARITY rattled off the last few words of the Path. Lab report, took the form out of the machine and reached for its cover. She was late by reason of Miss Hudson having to go to the dentist and Charity offering to finish off her reports for her. If she wasn't to keep Sidney waiting she would have to get a move on. She got to her feet, a tall shapely girl with curly dark hair pinned into a careless french pleat, and a pretty face, and stretched and yawned widely, glad to be free from her typewriter at last. She yawned again and crossed the bare little office to the minuscule cupboard where the pair of them hung their things and made the tea, and did her face and poked at her hair. Charity, a contented girl, sometimes found herself at the end of a busy day wishing that she was somewhere else; somewhere exotic, dressed to kill and being plied with champagne by some man who adored her . . . So silly, she admonished her reflection, and surely she was old enough not to daydream. Especially as there was Sidney. It was regrettable, but she had found herself quite unable to daydream about him. He was everything a prospective husband should be: non-smoking, non-drinking, with a steady job in a building society and a nice little nest egg; he was a pleasant companion, too. They had known each other for so long that she wasn't sure when the idea of marrying had turned from a vague possibility to a taken-for-granted fact. Certainly he had never actually proposed.

She fetched her purse from the desk drawer, turned

off the lamp and went out of the room, plunging at once into a narrow passage with a stone floor. It wound its way round the back of the hospital, a forgotten thoroughfare from Victorian times, only used by herself and Miss Hudson and anyone who delivered the reports, letters and treatment sheets, written for the most part in almost unreadable scrawls, which they deciphered and returned neatly typed, in an unending stream.

The familiar sounds of hospital life and the faint but penetrating smell of disinfectant, floor polish and Harpic, nicely blended, caused her to wrinkle her charming nose; she hardly noticed it during the day, but somehow by the time she left for home, it had become a bit much.

There were other people using the passage: porters, someone from X-Ray taking a short cut, a couple of nurses who shouldn't be there at all, and the nice little man who went round the wards collecting specimens. She greeted them all cheerfully, opened the door leading to the entrance hall and whipped smartly through it. The entrance hall was vast; the Victorians may have stinted on the gloomy semi-basement rooms and endless gloomier corridors, but they had let themselves go on the committee rooms, consultants' rooms and the entrance. From the outside, the front of the hospital resembled Euston Station, with more than a dash of the original Crystal Palace. The large glass doors opened on to a gloomy, marble-floored hall upon whose fairly lofty ceiling were depicted various scenes of a surgical or medical aspect, while round its dark oak-panelled walls stood an orderly row of dead and gone consultants, each on his plinth. Half-way down this symbol of Victorian ill-taste was the head porter's box, where old Mr Symes spent his days, ruling the porters with a heavy hand and a fount of knowledge when it came to the hospital and its activities. He knew the nursing staff, the students, the housemen and the consultants, and they in their turn regarded him as a kind of symbol; Augustine's without Symes was unthinkable.

He looked up from his paper as Charity crossed the waste of marble towards the door, wished her a civil good evening and then got to his feet and reached back to take a handful of notes from the board behind him. The glass doors had been thrust open and a man had come in: Professor Wyllie-Lyon, Senior Medical Consultant, a pleasant, rather quiet giant of a man about whom the hospital grapevine could find very little to say. No one knew if he were married or where he lived—no one being the nursing staff who found his good looks and great size irresistible.

He paused to take the messages Symes offered him, bade him a polite good evening and smiled at Charity. 'You work late, Miss Graham. Are we so hard on you?'

She stopped in front of him. 'Oh, no, sir, it's not that—Miss Hudson had the toothache and went to the dentist and there were one or two reports to finish.'

She smiled at him in return; she liked him. True, his notes and letters were sometimes scribbled in an abominable scrawl which took all her wits to decipher, and he had a nasty habit of springing something urgent on them to be typed just as they had cleared their desks for the day, but he was always beautifully mannered. She knew a good deal more about him than the grapevine, too, but discretion was part of her job. Sharing a table with the nurses at dinner time, she listened to them guessing as to where he lived or if he were married and, if so, to whom, knowing quite well that he had a house in an elegant backwater—an expensive one, too, she guessed—tucked away behind Wimpole Street; he wasn't married, either, but wild horses wouldn't have dragged that from her; he had mentioned it a while ago, quite casually, when he had brought some letters to be typed. His secretary, he had explained, was ill and would Charity be so kind? The letters had his home address but he had said nothing about that, only remarking before he went that he would collect them personally on the following day, 'For I shall be away for a day or so and my housekeeper will probably tidy them away if you post them.'

Now he didn't hurry away. 'You like your work?' he asked.

'Yes, very much; you see it isn't just office work; we meet lots of people—it's never boring.'

'You don't strike me as being a young lady to be easily bored.'

She was a little surprised at that. As far as she was aware he knew nothing about her; their meetings had been brief and businesslike.

'No, I'm not . . .'

'And now you will go to your home and doubtless spend your evening with some fortunate young man.' He stood in front of her, staring down into her face from heavy-lidded blue eyes.

'Well, yes.'

'Then I mustn't keep you.' He was his usual courteous self again and she bade him good night and went out into the chilly sombre autumn evening, feeling vaguely disturbed. She had no idea why and she shrugged the feeling off as she hurried along the crowded pavement to the bus stop.

She was already late and the next bus which came

along was already full; a precious ten minutes had passed before she squeezed on to the next one. Sidney would be put out at having to wait for her and would have to be soothed back into good spirits again. She frowned. It would be nice if he soothed her for a change, but somehow he always made her feel that she worked to please herself, without due regard to his feelings, and if she came home tired of an evening it was entirely her own fault. She had tried to explain to him when they had first started going out together, but she had sensed his lack of interest and had long ago dropped the subject. What was the use of explaining to him that although her father was a retired solicitor and tolerably comfortable, his propensity for buying rare books ate great holes into his income, and her aunt, who had come to live with them when her mother had died years ago, was incapable of being economical. She hadn't realised this herself until she had left school and found that there was to be no university because of lack of money. So she had taken a course of shorthand and typing, both of which she really didn't like, and found herself a job; it made her independent and in a year or two she could have found herself a small flat and lived her own life, but her aunt had come to depend on her contributions to the housekeeping and she was too kind-hearted a girl to ignore that.

She had been at St Augustine's for two years now and supposed that she would be there until Sidney asked her to marry him. She stood there, crammed between two men reading their evening papers, trying to imagine herself married to him. She still hadn't got the image right when she got off the bus at St John's Wood and walked briskly away from the Finchley Road down a sober side street. Her home was in the more unfashionable part, a modest semi-detached with a front garden hedged by laurel bushes and planted by her with daffodils, wallflowers and dahlias according to the season. In winter, alike with its neighbours, it was bare. Charity, who loved gardening, had done her best with chrysanthemums, but without much success. She stopped to look at them now, on her way up the garden path; they were soggy with October rain and damp, drooping against the sticks she had given them. For a few wild seconds she wanted to run away from London, to some quiet country spot where things grew, unhampered by soot and fog and neglect.

Sidney was in the sitting room with her aunt and she felt a wave of irritation when he didn't bother to get up as she went in, but only remarked on her lateness in what she called his civil servant's voice. She greeted her aunt and accorded him a 'Hallo', and stood a little uncertainly between them in the vaguely shabby room. The chairs needed new covers; if she didn't buy a new winter coat perhaps they could get some ... There were some nice pieces in the room: a canterbury and a davenport, a rent table in the window and a corner cupboard housing the Waterford glasses. She polished them all lovingly each weekend, but Aunt Emily didn't bother during the week. She took off her jacket and went to hang it in the hall, and Sidney said, 'I thought we were going out ... I've been waiting.' He sounded impatient.

'I had some work to finish; I'll only be ten minutes or so.'

'Too late to go to the cinema.'

She turned to look at him. 'The big film doesn't start until after eight o'clock.'

'Too late. I have to go to work in the morning—we can't all please ourselves.'

'I'm sure your work is very important,' observed Aunt Emily with a vague desire to please someone.

Sidney passed a hand over his pale hair and looked important. 'I hope I pull my weight,' he observed smugly. Charity, still standing at the door, knew for certain at that moment that she would never marry him. She gave a great sigh of relief; it was like a heavy weight falling away, or coming out of a mist into the bright sunshine. She was about to throw away her secure future, another semi-detached, suitably furnished—although at the rate Sidney was going, it would take some years. I'm twenty-six, she thought, and in ten years time I'll be thirty-six and very likely still living here. She said aloud, 'Then I'll make us all some coffee, shall I? Where's father?'

'In his study. A parcel of books came this morning.' Her aunt gave her an apologetic look. 'I believe there are some which he particularly wanted.'

Charity went along to the kitchen and made the coffee and cut the jam sponge she had made the evening before. She and Sidney usually had a snack supper when they went out together and she felt empty; when he had gone she would make a sandwich. She carried in the tray and pretended not to see his look of displeasure. Presently, she decided silently, she would walk to the corner of the street with him and tell him that she didn't want to see him again. She was by nature a kind-hearted girl, and careful not to hurt people's feelings, but she didn't think that Sidney would be hurt. Offended perhaps, annoyed because he'd have to look for another suitable wife, but not hurt.

She took in the coffee and her aunt poured it, aware that something was wrong but not sure what it was so that she embarked on a pointless conversation about nothing in particular until Sidney put down his cup and announced that he might as well go home.

'I'll walk with you to the corner,' said Charity and fetched her jacket, and Aunt Emily nodded and smiled, under the impression that whatever it was had blown over.

The corner wasn't far; Charity wasted no time but said at once, 'Sidney, I've been thinking—I'm not really what you want, you know. I think it would be a good idea if we didn't see each other again.' She glanced up at his face, lighted by a street lamp. 'We've known each other too long,' she finished flatly.

'You are throwing me over?' His voice was stiff with resentment.

'Well,' said Charity reasonably, 'I've never really had you, have I? I mean you've never said that you wanted to marry me—nor that you loved me.'

'There should be no need to state the obvious.' He was outraged.

'That's all very well, but do you love me, Sidney? And do just for once stop being a civil servant and be honest.'

'I have—did have—a deep regard for you, Charity.'

'But do you love me?' she persisted.

'If by that you mean . . .' He paused. 'No, I don't think that I do.' He added coldly, 'You would have been a most suitable wife.'

They had reached the corner. She said seriously, 'But that wouldn't have been enough for me, Sidney. I don't want to be a suitable wife, I want to be loved just because I'm me and not because I'm suitable. There's a difference, you know, although I'm not exactly sure what it is.'

Sidney gave a little sneering laugh. 'If you don't look out you'll be too old to find out. Goodbye, Charity.'

He turned on his heel and walked away and after a moment she walked back to her home and went indoors, back to the sitting room to her aunt, who said, 'Back so soon, my dear? I thought you and Sidney might be going to enjoy a pleasant stroll.'

'We're not going to see each other again,' said Charity clearly. 'It wouldn't have worked out. I'm sure he's a very good man and all that, but I'm not the wife for him—if ever he'd got around to asking me.'

'My dear Charity,' began Aunt Emily, and then, 'What will your father say?'

Charity was peering at herself in the handsome rococo mirror over the fireplace, poking her hair. 'Nothing much,' she said cheerfully. 'I don't think he liked Sidney very much, did he? And he's not really interested in me.'

Her aunt looked shocked. 'Charity! What a thing to say about your father.'

'Oh, I don't mean that he doesn't love me,' Charity explained. 'Just that there are other things which interest him more than I do.'

She turned away from the mirror. 'I expect I shall end up by being a spinster.'

'There must be a great many suitable young men at that hospital,' ventured Aunt Emily.

'Oh, plenty of young men,' agreed Charity, 'but they are not suitable. You see, that's the trouble—they're young. I'm twenty-six and all the older men I meet are already married.' She then remembered Professor Wyllie-Lyon, certainly not married but, she felt sure, a dyed-in-the-wool bachelor, content with his lectures and his seminars and his hospital rounds. 'Almost all,' she finished.

Her aunt looked so downcast that she bent to kiss

her cheek. 'I'll get supper shall I? I'm famished and Father will have to eat . . .'

She enjoyed cooking; that was one of the things Sidney had liked about her, being able to turn out appetising meals for a minimum cost. She set about making a cheese soufflé now and while it was in the oven laid the table in the small dining room, made even smaller by reason of the Regency oval table with its graceful ribbon-back chairs and the elegant sidetable which took up the whole of one wall. It was chilly there; she turned on the gas fire, drew the curtains and put on the white starched cloth her father insisted upon, then arranged the silver which had been in her mother's family for years and set out the glasses, for he liked his wine, too, even though it was supermarket claret.

The soufflé was ready and it would spoil unless they ate it at once. She urged her aunt to the table and went to fetch her father. He looked up as she went into the small room behind the dining room. 'Ah, my dear, have you had a good day? I have had a splendid parcel of books . . .'

She bent to kiss his elderly cheek. 'You have? That's nice. There is a soufflé in the oven waiting to be eaten—will you come now?'

He followed her reluctantly, poured the wine, and sat down while she shared out the soufflé. There was a salad, too, and they sat eating it, not talking much for her father's mind was on his books and Aunt Emily was still brooding over Sidney's departure. Charity, sitting between them, kept up a cheerful flow of small talk; she loved them both dearly, her elderly aunt and her elderly father. She couldn't remember them ever being young; her father had married in his late forties and her mother had been twenty years younger than

he, killed in a road accident when Charity had been six
years old. Aunt Emily had come then to look after
them both and, since she was only a year or so younger
than her brother, she had already been middle-aged;
they had done their best with the small girl, trying to
make up for the loss of her mother, and she had grown
up into a rather quiet young woman. She had had few
friends, for neither her father nor her aunt was
sociable and the few young men she had brought home
from time to time had been put off by her father's
bland disregard for their existence and her aunt's
insistence on making a third. It wasn't until she met
Sidney and had pointed out that she was getting on
towards thirty and quite able to look after herself that
they woke up to the fact that she was no longer a child.
They had even accepted his presence as a rather vague
future son-in-law. And now she had put paid to that in
no uncertain manner and, presently, she supposed she
might regret it.

She cleared the plates, put a bowl of fruit on the
table and fetched the coffee. Just one adventure, she
thought vividly, passing coffee cups; something really
exciting before she resigned herself to the quiet years
ahead. For they would be that. She was a pretty girl,
she knew that without conceit, but living such a
sheltered life for years had made her shy; she wished
she knew how to attract men, but she had very little
idea as to how to set about it. There had been no need
with Sidney, he had taken it for granted that she was
attracted to him and he had never expected to hear
anything else. Her thoughts were interrupted by her
aunt's gentle voice.

'I thought we might have fish tomorrow. Could you
get some, dear? I expect you can pop out during the
day . . .?'

Aunt Emily, never having had a job herself, had her own peculiar ideas about working hours.

Charity agreed at once. She had three-quarters of an hour for her lunch break, and there was a row of shops five minutes' walk away from Augustine's. Perhaps she would buy a sandwich and go and sit in the churchyard tucked away between the tatty streets. It was quiet there and, although the plane trees weren't very exciting, the grass grew between the ancient tombstones and there were birds, too.

The office looked dreary when she got there the next morning; it was a gloomy day with wild clouds scudding across the sky and the threat of rain, so that they had to have the lights on. Miss Hudson, minus the offending tooth and conscious of the gap which showed when she smiled, was disposed to be peevish, a state of affairs not improved by the pile of notes and letters already waiting to be typed.

Charity whipped off her typewriter cover, took the lion's share of work on to her desk, rolled paper and carbon into her machine and went to put the kettle on. 'You'll feel better after a cup of tea,' she promised and got out their mugs and the milk and sugar.

Miss Hudson sniffed. 'It's all very well for you young ones,' she grumbled, 'you don't have any worries.'

Charity didn't answer. Miss Hudson was within shouting distance of fifty, thin to the point of boniness, with a sharp nose and a sharp tongue and a refined voice. At least I won't be bony, thought Charity, looking down at her splendid curves and then worming her way into the cupboard to make the tea.

Refreshed, they worked without pause until Miss

Hudson looked at her watch. 'I'm off to the canteen,' she announced. 'You'll be all right, Charity?'

She always asked that; Charity had once or twice been tempted to say that, no, she wouldn't, and wondered what Miss Hudson would have to say to that. Left alone, she picked up one of Professor Wyllie-Lyon's reports and began to decipher it. The writing was worse than usual and there was an awful lot of it. She sighed gently. 'That anyone so clever could find it impossible to write so that anyone could read it!' she exclaimed to the room around her. 'And I wonder what that means—something something five times . . .'

'Sthenic,' said Professor Wyllie-Lyon in an apologetic voice.

She turned slowly to look at him standing in the doorway. He was holding another sheaf of papers, watching her and smiling at her a little. 'It means strong or active. The trouble is,' he went on, 'I can read my own writing and tend to forget that no one else can.'

He laid the papers on her desk. 'These are urgent, if you would be so kind?'

He was at the door again and she hadn't uttered a word. He was shutting it behind him when he put his head round to ask, 'I trust you had a pleasant evening, Miss Graham?'

'No,' said Charity and began to thump on her typewriter, stifling a sudden urge to tell him all about Sydney. She didn't look up as the door closed softly behind him.

Miss Hudson came back from her dinner in a better frame of mind. 'Run along,' she told Charity. 'Did anything else come in while I was away?'

'Another lot from Professor Wyllie-Lyon—urgent.'

Miss Hudson cast her eyes up to the ceiling. 'That man—nice though he is, and I'm sure I've never met anyone in this place with better manners—no wonder the nurses all fall for him. It's a pity he has to work so hard. I must leave on time, too; the dentist's going to take an impression . . .'

'I'll stay on if we are not finished,' offered Charity and thought uneasily of the fish. If she got the fishmonger to put it in a stout plastic bag and she put it on the windowsill and cooked it the moment she got home . . . Anyway it was quite a chilly day. She got her coat and started off along the passage. Five minutes to the shops, five minutes there, and she would buy a ham roll and eat it in the churchyard; there was a convenient cluster of old tombstones in one corner out of the wind. There would still be time to have a cup of coffee at the café at the end of the row of shops. Reg, the proprietor, made excellent coffee and one could ignore the plastic surroundings.

There was a queue at the fishmongers; she bought cod fillets and because she was a pretty girl with a nice smile the fishmonger wrapped them carefully in a second bag. She stowed the fish into her shopping basket, bought a ham roll and crossed the road to the churchyard.

There was no one else there; there seldom was. Sometimes in the summer she had found a tramp sleeping peacefully on one of the stone slabs, and once or twice someone like herself, intent on peace and quiet for half an hour. She selected an eighteenth-century angel to lean against and began on her roll.

She had scarcely sunk her splendid teeth into it before someone came strolling towards her. Professor Wyllie-Lyon, hands in pockets and just for once no papers that needed typing immediately. She paused, the roll half-way to her open mouth; surely he hadn't sought her out to do some urgent notes?

It seemed not. He came to a halt in front of her and remarked pleasantly, 'We seem to share the same desire for peace and quiet, Miss Graham. May I sit for a moment?'

He arranged his great size against the scroll over which the angel was brooding. The family Wodecock: father, mother and a quiverful of children; there were so many of them that the scroll made an excellent support for such a large man. After a moment he said, 'Fish?'

She watched his magnificent nose flare. 'Well, yes, I've just bought some for supper when I get home.'

'Ah, yes, of course. Do go on with your lunch, Miss Graham. I come here to close my eyes for ten minutes—it's quiet.'

A hint for her not to talk? She took another bite of her roll. His eyes were still shut when she had finished. She brushed the crumbs away and got soundlessly to her feet and he was there, beside her, wide awake, looming over her.

'I would be glad if you would have a cup of coffee with me, Miss Graham. Reg, at the café by the grocer's, makes a splendid cup.'

'Yes, I go there sometimes—it's a change from the canteen.' She discovered to her surprise that she didn't feel shy with him. 'Thank you, I've just got the time before half past one.'

They were sitting at an orange, plastic-topped table, their coffee before them, before he asked, 'What went wrong then?'

She was an honest girl; it didn't occur to her to pretend she didn't know what he was talking about. She said, 'Oh, I'm still not sure.' She was silent for so long that she heard him say comfortably, 'I dare say it will sort itself out.'

And she had been on the point of telling him all about it. She must be mad, she thought crossly; she didn't even know the man. They didn't move in the same hospital circles and she felt pretty sure that their social backgrounds were as wide apart as the poles. He was being kind without making much of an effort, probably because he knew that it was he, more than any of the other consultants, who kept her nose to the grindstone.

She drank her coffee, glanced at her watch, thanked him and got up to go. He got up, too, but made no effort to accompany her. His goodbye was impersonal and casual. She went back to the hospital feeling peevish.

Miss Hudson, as always, glanced at the clock as she went in. They worked well together, but she let it be known by small signs such as this that she was in charge. 'Dr Carruthers'—she bridled a little, for she fancied him—'popped in with a couple of letters. There's not much else besides Professor Wyllie-Lyon's stuff, is there?'

Luckily not, thought Charity, hanging up her coat, for there was more than enough of it.

She was a little more than half-way through them when Miss Hudson fancied a cup of tea and while Charity was filling the kettle the phone rang. 'That was to ask you to take the professor's papers down to the consultants' room should they not be ready by five o'clock.'

Miss Hudson inserted a fresh sheet of paper. 'Will you be done by then?'

'No,' said Charity, 'I had those biopsy reports to do, you know.' She made the tea and carried the tray to

Miss Hudson's desk. 'I'm about half-way. It'll be six o'clock I should think.'

'Poor you,' said Miss Hudson, not meaning it. She sipped her tea in a genteel fashion. 'I did hear a rumour that he was off shortly on some lecturing tour or other; that'll make life much easier for us both.'

Which, seeing that she had long ago left Charity to deal with almost all of his work, wasn't quite true.

The office seemed very quiet when Miss Hudson had gone. The afternoon was already darkening and there was a first splattering of rain against the uncurtained windows. Charity remembered the fish wedged on the windowsill and brought it inside, then settled down to work again. Another hour's work, she reckoned, perhaps less since there would be no interruptions now. The administrative side of Augustine's had packed up and gone home, leaving the nurses to their work; she could hear faint hospital sounds and from time to time the strident warning of an ambulance.

She finished before an hour was up, tidied her desk and put on her coat and picked up her work. There was no one in the passage; the day's rush had died down for the moment, patients were being readied for their suppers; except for the non-stop flow of patients in the accident room, Augustine's was, for a little while, tolerably quiet.

Charity hurried along, anxious to get home; Aunt Emily would be worrying about supper. She gained the entrance hall and turned down one of the corridors leading from it, wider than the rest, lined by magnificent mahogany doors. This was where the consultants, the management committee and the upper heirarchy of the hospital had their various rooms. The consultants' was half-way down; she tapped at the door and went in. Professor Wyllie-Lyon was overflowing a chair with his feet on the table. He appeared to be sleeping, but as she hesitated he said, 'Come on in. I'm much obliged to you, Miss Graham; I've curtailed your evening.'

He had taken his large feet in his handmade shoes off the table and was looming over her. 'It was important that I should have these,' he observed as he took the papers she handed him. 'They need to be delivered this evening.'

Charity murmured a nothing, said good night and made for the door. He reached it first, which was surprising considering that he was such a large man and so far away from it.

'I'll drop you off,' he said and when she said, 'Oh, there's no need of that,' he interrupted her gently, 'You live in St John's Wood; I'm going in that direction. It's the least I can do.'

'But it's my work,' protested Charity.

He took no notice of that, but gathered up the papers and opened the door and ushered her through. Short of making a silly fuss there was nothing she could do but accompany him out of the hospital and into the dark blue Bentley parked in the forecourt.

The professor, beyond a word here and there, had little to say as he drove along the Finchley Road. Presently he asked, 'Where do I turn off?'

'Oh, this will do, thank you,' said Charity. 'I can walk down here—it's quite close . . .'

'In that case I'll drive you there.'

He had the reputation of being quite mild at the hospital, but she had the feeling that that was a cover-up for a steely determination to get his own way. After all, how many dozens of times had she meekly agreed to type his letters, knowing that she had no hope of finishing them by five o'clock when she was supposed to go home? She gave him her address and sat silently until he stopped outside the gate. He leaned across and opened the door for her. 'Forgive me if I don't get out; time is of the essence.'

It was on the tip of her tongue to point out that he could have saved himself a few minutes by dropping her off in the Finchley Road when she had suggested it, but all she said was a polite thank you and a rather brisk good night, uneasily aware that the cod might have left a faintly fishy atmosphere in his beautiful car. She was surprised that he didn't drive away until she had gone through the gate and shut it behind her.

Aunt Emily came into the hall to meet her; she might be elderly but her hearing was excellent. 'I heard a car,' she began. 'Have you and Sidney made it up, darling?' And, before Charity could reply, 'You bought the fish?'

'Yes, Aunt Emily—it's here. I'll take it straight to the kitchen. And yes, you did hear a car, but it wasn't Sidney and we haven't made it up. It was one of the consultants at St Augustine's—I stayed late to finish some work for him and he gave me a lift as he was coming this way.'

Upon reflection she wondered if that had been true. The papers had been urgent—reports on a case of leukaemia he had been consulted about, but the patient, if she remembered aright, had been in an East End hospital in exactly the opposite direction. He had said that he had needed the reports urgently, but if that was the case why had he wasted time bringing her home? Perhaps he had some other urgent business to attend to first.

She didn't bother her head over it but went to say

hallo to her father and then started on the fish.

In the oven with a bit of parsley, she decided; easy to prepare and not too long to cook. While it was cooking she sat down at the kitchen table with her aunt. As so often happened, that lady had used up the housekeeping money and shied away from asking her brother for more until it was due. 'I do try to be economical, dear,' she observed worriedly, 'but somehow the money just goes . . .'

Charity, who had had her eye on a pair of expensive shoes for some weeks and had intended to buy them on pay-day, heaved an inward sigh. By the time she had enough money for them they wouldn't be fashionable any more. She wasn't extravagant and she didn't buy many clothes, but what she had were good and suited her, for she bought with a careful eye. She said now, 'Don't worry, Aunty, I've a few pounds tucked away—you can pay me back later.' They both knew that that wouldn't happen but neither of them mentioned the fact.

At supper her father remarked, 'You came home by car, Charity? I was at my window . . .'

She told him about the professor, but only briefly, for half-way through he interrupted with, 'Ah, that reminds me, in the catalogue I had sent to me today there's a book I think I must have: early medical practices in Europe; it should be most informative. This professor would doubtless be very interested.'

Very unlikely, thought Charity, murmuring agreement. Just for a moment, as she changed the plates, she wondered where he was and what he was doing at that moment. Wining and dining some exquisite young lady, or with his head buried in some dry-as-dust tome? Probably the latter, propped up against the cruet while he ate his solitary dinner.

Charity, who had a very vivid imagination, felt rather sorry for him, allowing her imagination to run away with her common sense, as she so often did.

CHAPTER TWO

Miss Hudson's rumour must have had some truth in it, for Charity saw nothing of Professor Wyllie-Lyon for the whole of the following week. It made her workload much lighter, of course, but she found herself missing him. She went home each evening to spend it in the company of her aunt and father and an occasional visitor, dropping in for a drink or after-supper coffee. True, she could have gone out on at least two occasions, once with the assistant dispenser, a short earnest young man with no sense of humour, and on the second occasion with the surgical registrar, who was married with a wife and family somewhere in the depths of rural Sussex. She had declined both invitations in her pleasant, rather shy manner and found herself wondering what she would have done if it had been Professor Wyllie-Lyon who had asked her out. Leapt at the chance, she had to admit, and then told herself sternly that she was being silly; for one thing he wasn't there and for another he had never been known to date anyone at the hospital. Even at the annual ball, which she had attended on two occasions, he had circled the floor with grave dignity with the senior ladies present and then gone to play bridge in an adjoining room.

She did the shopping on Saturday morning, met an acquaintance unexpectedly and had coffee with her, and then walked unhurriedly back home, to come face to face with Sidney when she was half-way there. He had a girl with him, someone she knew slightly, and

they both looked embarrassed, whereas she felt
nothing but pleased relief that Sidney should have
found a successor to herself so quickly. Once or twice
she had felt guilty about him, but now she saw that
there was no need for that. She beamed at them both,
passed the time of day and went on her way with her
groceries to give a hand with the lunch and then catch
a bus to visit an old school friend who had married
and gone to live in Putney.

Sunday held no excitement either; church in the
morning and then an afternoon in the garden,
encouraging the chrysanthemums and tidying up the
flower beds for the winter. Charity, restless for no
reason at all, was quite glad to go to work on Monday
morning.

Miss Hudson was in a bad temper; she had missed
her usual bus, lost her umbrella and started a cold.
Charity hurried to put on the kettle and offer a soothing
cup to cheer while she sorted through the pile of work
waiting for them. There was quite a lot. She accepted
the major portion of reports since, as she was quick to
point out, Miss Hudson didn't feel able to cope, and
they settled down to a morning's work.

They were interrupted after an hour or so by
Symes's elderly voice growling over the phone. Would
Miss Graham take her notebook to Women's Medical,
as Professor Wyllie-Lyon wanted notes taken during
his round.

Miss Hudson was indignant. 'Leaving me alone
here to get through all this pile of work. I shall have
something to say about it, I can tell you! You'd better
get along at once, Charity, and be sure you are back in
time for me to go to the canteen. I feel very poorly and
it is essential that I have a break.'

Charity gathered up her notebook and pencil. It

would make a nice change from the typewriter; besides, she would see Professor Wyllie-Lyon again. She didn't waste time in wondering why she was pleased about this but nipped smartly along the passage, into the entrance hall and up the stairs. She wasn't supposed to use the main staircase but it would take all day to go round to either of the smaller staircases used by the nurses, and the lifts were out of the question. Anyway, she disliked lifts.

The round had started; Charity, peering cautiously round the ward doors, met Sister's frowning gaze and then, obedient to her beckoning finger, and very aware of her size and bursting good health, walked just as cautiously down the ward between the beds occupied by a variety of limp-looking ladies with pale faces who gazed at her with a kind of disbelief that anyone could be as pretty and full of life. Miss Hudson would have been more suitable, thought Charity, gaining the group of solemn-looking people round a patient's bed, and doing her best to hide herself behind the social worker.

'Ah, good morning, Miss Graham,' observed Professor Wyllie-Lyon, yards away from her and with eyes in the back of his head. 'If you will be ready to take notes at the next patient's bed, if you please.'

He hadn't turned round as he spoke, so that she addressed his white-coated back with a polite, 'Certainly, sir,' while admiring what she could see of him—which wasn't much, what with his registrar and housemen and a clutch of earnest medical students. Sister had the best place, of course, at his elbow, ready with X-Rays, forms and the proper answers to his questions. Charity wondered what it would be like to be clever enough to know what he was talking about and what to say in reply. She allowed her thoughts to wander. It was a pity that she was really too old to train as a nurse, although she wasn't sure if she would be much good at it—the actual nursing that is; she enjoyed learning about the various conditions and ailments she typed about each day, but she wasn't so sure about the practical side of them.

She became aware that there was a general movement towards the next bed and hastily held her pencil at the ready. A good thing, too, for Professor Wyllie-Lyon began at once. 'Now, this is Mrs Elliott, whose case we might discuss, with her permission.' He sat himself down on the side of the bed and spoke to the elderly lady lying in it. She smiled and nodded and he then turned to address the students round him.

'You are ready, Miss Graham? Now, this patient is suffering from a comparatively rare complaint . . .'

Charity, standing close by so that she wouldn't miss anything, kept her mind on her work. And again, a good thing that she did; she was grateful when he paused to ask her if she had got Thrombocytopenic Purpura down correctly. A few more tongue twisters like that and she would throw her notebook at him and gallop out of the ward.

She hoped that she had got everything down correctly, as she hurried back to the office; Miss Hudson would be in a fine state, for she was missing part of her dinner time. Charity, short of breath from running down the passage, was greeted by her irate superior, even more irate by reason of the delightful picture Charity made: cheeks pink from her haste, her magnificent bosom heaving.

'Ten minutes,' snapped Miss Hudson. 'I said to be back on time . . .'

'Well,' said Charity reasonably, 'I couldn't just walk

away before Professor Wyllie-Lyon had finished, could I? I've run all the way back.'

Miss Hudson sniffed. 'I shall take the ten minutes out of your dinner time. I don't see why I should suffer. Really, you young women, you have no sense of responsibility.' She flounced out, leaving Charity to make sense of this, and since she couldn't she sat down at her desk, polished off the Path. Lab reports awaiting her attention and then turned to her shorthand notes. Professor Wyllie-Lyon hadn't said that he wanted them at once but she had no doubt that he did.

Miss Hudson was as good as her word. She came back ten minutes late, viewed the fresh pile of work which the porter had just brought to the office with a jaundiced eye and asked, 'Have you finished those notes, then? There's more than enough to keep us busy until five o'clock.'

The phone rang and she answered it, then said crossly, 'You're to take Professor Wyllie-Lyon's notes down to Women's Medical as soon as they're ready. I must say he's got a nerve . . .'

'He is the senior consultant,' Charity pointed out in her reasonable way. 'I expect he's got the edge on everyone else. Anyway, I've almost finished; I'll drop them in as I go to dinner.'

'Toad-in-the-hole,' said Miss Hudson, 'and they've overcooked the cabbage again.'

Charity, who was famished, would have eaten it raw.

Women's Medical was settling down for the afternoon. There was the discreet clash of bedpans, scurrying feet intent on getting done so that their owners could go off duty, and the faint cries of such ladies who required this, that or the other before they could settle for their hour's rest period. Charity knocked on Sister's office door and went in.

Sister was at her desk. She was a splendid nurse and a dedicated spinster with cold blue eyes and no sense of humour. Her ward was run beautifully and her nurses disliked her whole-heartedly.

Professor Wyllie-Lyon was sitting opposite her, perched precariously on a stool much too small to accommodate his vast person. He looked up as Charity went in, put down the notes he was reading and got to his feet. Sister gave him a surprised look.

'What do you want, Miss Graham?' she asked.

'I was told to leave these notes, Sister.'

The professor took them from her. 'Ah, yes. Splendid. Good girl. You never let me down, do you? But shouldn't you be at your dinner?'

'Oh, that's all right, Professor. I'm on my way now . . .'

'It is desirable for the smooth running of the hospital catering department that staff should be punctual at mealtimes,' interrupted Sister severely.

'In that case, Miss Graham, run and get your coat and we'll go and find a sandwich somewhere. I'm even more unpunctual than you are.'

Sister's disapproval was tangible. 'That does not apply to you, Professor Wyllie-Lyon, although I'm sure that you are joking.'

He was at the door, waiting for a bemused Charity to go through it.

'No, no. How could I joke about such an important matter? I must set a good example, must I not? I'll be back during the afternoon, Sister, and thank you.'

On the landing Charity said, 'That was very . . .' And then she closed her mouth with a snap and blushed.

'Go on,' he encouraged.

She shook her head. 'I'm sorry, I forgot who you were; I can't say things like that to senior consultants, I'd get the sack.'

He was propelling her gently away from the ward. 'No, you won't—I promise I won't tell.'

She shook her head again, suddenly shy. 'I must go—I'm late . . .'

He said patiently, 'Well, we've already discussed that, haven't we? Get your coat, there's a good girl, I'm very hungry.'

'Yes, but . . .'

'I shall call you Charity, a pleasant name. Also I still haven't been told what went wrong.' He gave her a gentle shove and she went back to the office and fetched her coat, muttered about shopping to an inquisitive Miss Hudson, and found him waiting where she had left him.

She was quite sure that she was doing something absolutely outrageous in the eyes of such as Miss Hudson or the sister on Women's Medical. Prudence urged her to make an excuse and go to the canteen, but for once she turned a deaf ear; it struck her with some force that life, as she lived it, was becoming increasingly dull and she was shocked to discover at the same time that Sidney had done nothing to enliven it. Looking at the large man standing beside her, it seemed likely that he might brighten it, even if only for half an hour. She smiled with sudden brilliance at him and he blinked.

'No time for a decent meal,' he observed pleasantly as they went down to the entrance and, under old Symes's eye, crossed the hall. 'There's a tolerable pub round the corner where we might get a decent sandwich. You don't mind a pub?'

Sidney had never taken her into one; ladies, he had said, never went into bars.

'The Cat and Fiddle? Where all the students go? The nursing staff aren't allowed . . .' She beamed at him. 'But I'm not a nurse . . .'

'And I hope never will be.' They were walking along the busy pavement and he took her arm to guide her down a side street.

She said worriedly, 'Oh, would I be so bad at it? I wondered if I might train—I'm a bit old . . .'

She was annoyed when he answered placidly. 'Far too old. But you'd like to change your job?'

'Well, yes. The work is interesting but I never see anyone but Miss Hudson.'

'And me.' He opened the pub door and ushered her inside the saloon bar, empty but for a handful of sober types drinking Guinness and eating something in a basket.

The professor swept her to a table in the corner, sat her down and asked, 'Drinks—what will you have?'

She found his company exhilarating. Gin and tonic, which she never drank, would have been appropriate. 'Oh, coffee, if I can have it—I've a mass of work this afternoon.'

He smiled gently. 'So have I. Sandwiches, or something in a basket?'

'Sandwiches, please. I cook a meal when I get home in the evening.'

'After a day's work?' He sounded vaguely interested, no more.

'Oh, I like cooking.' She looked away so that he wouldn't ask any more questions and he went over to the bar to give their order.

They didn't talk much as they ate; they hadn't

enough time for that, but over their coffee he asked, 'So what went wrong?'

He didn't give up easily, thought Charity, and she was wondering how to get out of telling him when he went on, 'Consider me as an elder brother or an uncle.' And somehow he contrived to look either the one or the other.

She glanced at her watch; there were still ten minutes left.

'Well, there is nothing to tell. I suddenly knew that I didn't want to go on sort of waiting for Sidney. I mean there wasn't anything definite; I suppose we'd just drifted into taking it for granted that we'd marry one day.' She sighed. 'I got home late and he didn't like having to wait for me . . .'

'I think that's my fault. I gave you that extra work.'

'Not your fault at all,' said Charity with some spirit. 'If it hadn't been you it could have been anyone else. It's my job, isn't it?'

Professor Wyllie-Lyon sat back in his chair as though he had nothing to do for the rest of the day. 'Do you ever feel that you would like to change your job, Charity?'

She said seriously, 'Oh, yes, but what could I do? I'm nothing but a shorthand typist, you know.'

'A good one, if I may say so. But you are a capable young woman, you can cook and presumably keep house and you get on well with people, don't you?'

She said with sudden fierceness. 'I want to travel, see other countries; soon it will be too late.' She stopped, ashamed of her outburst, but he didn't seem to notice that.

'You would like to marry and have children?'

'Oh, yes.' She was off again, speaking her thoughts aloud. 'A large rambling house with a huge garden and dogs and cats and a donkey and children—not just one or two.' She stopped for a second time, going slowly pink under his gaze, wondering what had come over her, talking such nonsense to someone she hardly knew. 'I really must get back,' she said, with a briskness which brought a quiver to the professor's mouth.

He agreed unfussily and talked of nothing much on their brief journey back to the hospital, and at the door he thanked her pleasantly for her company and hoped that her afternoon wouldn't be too busy.

She darted down the passage, her thoughts a fine muddle. She had enjoyed being with him, she liked him; on the other hand she had allowed her tongue to run away with her. Perhaps he had been bored? She burst into the office, blushing furiously at the very idea, so that Miss Hudson gave her a surprised look and said with unwonted concern, 'Well, there's no need to break your neck, dear. You're scarlet from hurrying. You'd better have a drink of water.' She glanced at the clock. 'You're not late.'

Charity looked rather wildly at her. 'Oh, good—I rather forgot the time.' She hung her coat in the cupboard, obediently drank a glass of water and went to her desk. A lot of reports had come in while she had been away and, as usual, she had the lion's share. Not that she minded; the more she had to occupy her, the better, and in future she would keep out of Professor Wyllie-Lyon's way.

She had no need to worry; there was no sign of him. And a very good thing too, she told herself severely; she was becoming far too interested in him. She had to remind herself of this several times during the following week; the days seemed long and purposeless and her quiet evenings at home excessively dull. She welcomed Saturday at last, with the prospect of the Church Fête, an annual affair which tried everyone connected with it to their utmost. Weeks ago she had agreed to help her aunt with a stall: fancy goods, which meant handiwork done by the ladies of the parish. She spent Saturday morning arranging tea cosies, hand-painted calendars, embroidered tray-clothes, aprons and a variety of crochet work, some items of which she was unable to recognise.

She and Aunt Emily hurried back home for a hasty lunch and then presented themselves, in the nick of time, before the church hall doors opened to the public to allow the small crowd in. Most of them made for the jumble stall, crowding round it impatiently while a film star of the lesser kind made an opening speech. Charity, re-arranging knitted egg cosies, listened with half an ear. The star had a faint lisp, which became irksome after a few minutes, but she received hearty applause, although whether that was because she had finished talking and everyone could get down to the business in hand, or because they admired her oration, was a moot point.

Talking animatedly to the vicar, she did a round of the stalls, but not of course the jumble, and left presently, the richer by a number of useless articles she didn't want, and almost totally unnoticed by the audience she had so recently addressed.

Charity, persuading a haughty lady from the better end of St John's Wood to buy a crocheted bedjacket in a revolting pink, had just taken the money and popped the garment into a bag before she could change her mind, when she looked up and saw Professor Wyllie-Lyon, head and shoulders above everyone else, coming towards her. She handed change, assured the lady that she would never regret her purchase and, swallowing back pleasure at the sight of him, wished him what she hoped was a cool good afternoon.

He didn't bother to answer that. 'Is this how you spend your leisure?' he wanted to know. 'I must say you have remarkably persuasive powers; no woman worth her salt would wear a pink monstrosity such as you have just sold her.'

'This is a bazaar; people buy things they don't want—it's quite usual.' She re-arranged some baby bootees in sky-blue. 'How—how did you get here?'

'By car.'

'Oh, well, yes. Of course. I mean, do you know anyone here?'

'You.'

'Oh, I thought—that is, have you been away, Professor?'

'Ah—you missed me.' He smiled in a self-satisfied way so that she felt impelled to say, 'I missed all the work.'

'You sound tart.' He looked around him. 'How long does this go on for?'

'Until half-past five.' She became aware that Aunt Emily was sidling towards her end of the stall, intent on being introduced. She said clearly, 'Aunt, this is Professor Wyllie-Lyon from the hospital—my aunt, Miss Graham.'

She had always thought of him as being a reserved man, very large and learned, and with a mind way above church bazaars and the like; she had been wrong. He listened with every sign of interest to her aunt's rambling discourse encompassing church bazaars in general, her own stall in particular and the amount of work it involved. 'Although of course it would be far harder if it wasn't for Charity's help— such a dear girl; a real support to her father and myself.' Aunt Emily, quite carried away, went on, 'Such a pity about Sidney, you know. We quite thought . . .'

Charity's voice throbbed with feeling, even though it was quiet. 'I don't expect that the professor is interested.'

Aunt Emily prided herself on being able to take a hint. 'Of course, dear, how foolish of me.' She peered up at him, studying his impassive face. 'I dare say you're very clever and learned—Charity's father is, you know—a bookworm, as I so often tell him. I like a nice romantic novel myself, but he prefers first editions . . .'

'Indeed?' Professor Wyllie-Lyon had focused all his attention on Aunt Emily. 'A man after my own heart; I'm a collector myself.'

Aunt Emily beamed. 'Well, but how interesting; you must come and meet my brother, I'm sure you would have a lot in common.

The professor's eyes rested briefly on Charity's face. 'I believe that we have.'

Charity, counting out change to a very pregnant young woman who had bought three pairs of bootees, stretched her ears, anxious not to miss a word.

'If you are free this evening?' began Aunt Emily. 'We close the bazaar in half an hour—perhaps you would care to come back with us and meet my brother? I'm sure he'll be delighted.'

The professor's heavy-lidded eyes took in the look of consternation on Charity's face and he smiled very faintly. 'That would be delightful,' he observed blandly. 'I have my car outside; may I give you a lift? I'll be outside when you are ready to leave.'

He took his leave, gave Charity a casual nod, and wandered off to try his luck on the bottle stall.

'Such a nice man,' declared her aunt. She turned rather vague blue eyes on to Charity's. 'So easy to talk to. Do you see much of him, my dear?'

Charity was totting up the takings. 'Very little, Aunty, although I do see a great deal of his work.' She added worriedly, 'I can't think how he got here.'

'By car, dear,' said her aunt, adding, 'So nice to get a lift home; my feet ache.'

The bazaar wound itself to a close, the last stragglers left, the takings were handed over to the vicar and the contents of the stalls were bundled into bags and boxes, to be stored until the summer fête next year—proceedings which took very little time, for the various ladies who had manned the stalls were longing for their tea. All the same, Charity and her aunt were among the last to leave, for the latter could never resist a quick gossip, with her friends. He'll be gone, thought Charity gloomily as they went out into the October dusk. But he wasn't; he was sitting in his car, showing no sign of impatience. He got out when he saw them, ushered them both into the back and drove the short distance through the quiet suburban streets.

'Here we are,' declared Aunt Emily, quite un-necessarily. 'Do come in. Did you have tea? I shall make some at once, for we had none, although I dare say you would prefer a drink with my brother.'

Charity, following her aunt into the house and then standing on one side while that lady ushered him in, didn't look at him. She felt awkward in a situation thrust upon her; probably the professor had absolutely no wish to meet her father. After all, there was no earthly reason why he should, even if he did collect books. She had the awful feeling that Aunt Emily had seized the opportunity to invite him under the impression that he might be Mr Right. Charity squirmed at the thought; her aunt had been going on for years about Mr Right and just for a little while Sidney had filled the bill; now she would start her well-meant matchmaking again.

She murmured a nothing and sidled into the kitchen to get the tea. Pray heaven that, by the time it was ready, he would be in her Father's study drinking whisky or, better still, on the point of departure.

Neither of those hopes was to be fulfilled. Professor Wyllie-Lyon was sitting, very much at his ease, in the sitting room with her aunt on one side of him and her father on the other. Her aunt was taking no part in the conversation, understandably, for the two gentlemen were discussing Homer's works and arguing pleasantly over which of the seven cities had the honour of being his birthplace. They paused, however, while Aunt Emily handed tea and cake and chatted about her afternoon. 'Very successful,' she declared in tones of satisfaction. 'Was it not, Charity?'

Charity agreed; she had had very little to say and now her father observed with vague kindness, 'A pleasant afternoon out for you, my dear; I'm sure you enjoyed it.'

She said that, Oh, yes, she had, and got up to fill the teapot, and presently the two men excused themselves on the plea that there was a particularly fine first edition her father wished to show to his guest. Charity, listening to them prosing on about Homer, tossing bits of poems in the original Greek to and fro, felt rising frustration. She must be tired, she decided, clearing away the tea things and conferring with her aunt as to what they should have for supper.

'Do you suppose he'll stay?' wondered Aunt Emily hopefully. 'There's that quiche you made this morning, dear, and we could have a salad and biscuits and cheese.'

'He won't stay,' said Charity.

It was her father who put his head round the kitchen door to inform them that Professor Wyllie-Lyon would be staying for supper; most fortunately he had declared that he had nothing much to do that evening, and it was a splendid opportunity to leaf through the Walter Scott first edition her father had been fortunate enough to pick up that week.

Charity sighed and began to prepare the salad. The professor had been a kind of secret delight to her, an interest in her otherwise rather staid life, but that was all. She had never imagined him even remotely associated with her life; indeed, she considered it highly unlikely that he would welcome the idea. It was obvious to her that they came from different backgrounds, their only mutual interest being the hospital. Why or how he had come to visit the bazaar was something she couldn't begin to guess at. That was bad enough; what was worse was having him here, in the house. With regret she had to admit that things wouldn't be the same again.

She sliced tomatoes and began to arrange them in a neat pattern on the lettuce, to stop suddenly at the awful thought that he might imagine that, because he'd had tea at her home, he would need to be friendly at the hospital. Of course, he had always been that in an austere kind of way, but now he might feel under an obligation. Her cheeks grew hot and her aunt, coming to see how the salad was going, remarked with some concern that she looked feverish.

She had worked herself into a state for nothing; at supper Professor Wyllie-Lyon behaved towards her as he had always done—friendly in a casual, slightly absent-minded way, placidly eating his supper, keeping the conversational ball rolling without once taking control of it, giving anyone who hadn't met him the impression that he was a friend of the family who had dropped in for a pleasant evening.

She bore the remains of their meal away to the kitchen and took coffee into the sitting room, and presently he got up to go with the remark that Mr Graham must at some time visit him so that he might browse through his library. His leave-taking of Miss Graham was everything that lady could have wished for, and as for Charity, she was swept to the front door and was not quite sure how she had got there.

'A very pleasant evening,' said the professor and waited, his eyes on her face.

'Why did you come?' It sounded a bit bald, but she wasn't a girl to mince her words.

'Ah, as to that I am not absolutely certain myself, so I am unable to answer you for the moment. Later perhaps?' He smiled gently down at her, and it struck her how nice it was for someone to actually look down at her; so often, being a tall girl, she was forced to dwindle into her shoes when she was talking to someone. 'Your father is something of a scholar. A most enjoyable conversation.'

She asked abruptly: 'Have you any friends?'

'Oh, lord! Too many—and I neglect them shamefully. I so seldom have any free time . . .'

'This afternoon . . .' She was so anxious to get to the bottom of his visit that she had forgotten to be shy.

'Well, as to that . . . a sudden whim, shall we say?' He held out a large hand and shook hers gently. 'Enjoy your weekend,' he observed in a non-committal voice which told her nothing, and he went down the garden path to his car. She stood there, watching him drive away, and found herself looking forward to Monday.

Which, as it turned out, was just like any other day! Miss Hudson still moaning on about her lost umbrella and the remnants of her cold; no central heating because the engineers were having a meeting to decide if they could take industrial action over something or other; and a load of reports waiting to be typed.

'The Path. Lab must have been working overtime at the weekend,' grumbled Miss Hudson. 'Of course they get double time if they do. I have a good mind to go on strike myself.' She sniffed in a ladylike fashion. 'Charity, you'll have to change your dinner hour with me. I've a dental appointment.'

'More teeth?' Charity asked, her mind on other things.

'You have no need to be funny at my expense,' said Miss Hudson huffily. 'I'll do Dr Clarkson's ledgers, you can get on with those reports.'

Dr Clarkson's correspondence was always commendably brief and, what was more, written clearly; some of the reports had presumably been scribbled by a spider. Charity sighed, and attacked the first; it was full of long words, like cephalhaematoma and cinchocaine hydrochloride, which hadn't been written clearly in the first place and which she couldn't spell anyway. By twelve o'clock she was glad to go to her dinner.

The meal was unappetising; presumably the engineers' meeting had disorganised the kitchens as well, for slabs of corned beef, baked beans and instant mashed potato were offered on a take-it or leave-it basis. Charity, sharing a table with several theatre nurses who were discussing the morning's list in colourful detail, wished she had goine to Reg's café,

but if she had done that she might have missed
Professor Wyllie-Lyon. The thought sprung unbidden
into her mind and she made haste to bury it under the
grim details concerning a patient's gangrenous ap-
pendix. All the same, it would brighten a dull day if he
were to bring his letters to the office . . .

Which he had done while she was in the canteen.

'No hurry for that lot,' explained Miss Hudson,
nodding at the little pile he had left on her desk while
she titivated herself for her own dinner. 'And I must
say, that's unusual. And X-Ray came up for that
report about the man with multiple injuries—you
hadn't done it—I had to interrupt my own work . . .'

Charity sat down at her desk, disappointment
welling slowly inside her; a good-natured girl, she was
suddenly peevish.

'I've had to do the same for you often enough,' she
snapped, and flung paper into her machine, taking no
notice of Miss Hudson's gasp of surprise.

'Well!' said that lady. 'Well! I have never been
spoken to like that in all my years here. I must say,
Charity, if that is to be your attitude you might do
better in another job.'

She flounced away and Charity pounded away at
her reports. Another job might be an idea, give her a
fresh outlook on life; but work was hard to come by
these days and her salary was needed at home. It
would need a miracle.

It seemed that they still occurred; the door opened
and Professor Wyllie-Lyon came in without haste.
'Ah, good morning, or is it afternoon?' He bent an
intent eye on her still-cross face. 'I wondered if you
would consider giving up your job here and coming to
work for me?'

CHAPTER THREE

CHARITY, both hands poised above the keys, allowed her gentle mouth to drop open, while she gazed at the professor. 'What did you say?' she managed finally.

He repeated himself patiently as he closed the door behind him.

'Me?' asked Charity. 'Work for you?'

'My dear girl, do stop looking as though you are concussed.'

'Why?'

His eyebrows lifted slightly. 'I feel that you would be most suitable. You are normally a calm, hard-working young woman, able to write accurate shorthand and type rapidly. You can also spell. My secretary is leaving to get married and I need to replace her; you have mentioned that you might enjoy a change of occupation. These two facts might possibly combine to make a satisfactory whole.'

'Well,' said Charity, and again, 'Well . . . I think I might like that—only I'm working here . . .'

'I am aware of that. You are subject to one month's notice on either side. My secretary leaves in less than five weeks' time, which gives you time in which to give in your notice and work with her for a few days in order to get some idea of the work involved.'

His smile was so encouraging that she smiled widely. 'Must I decide now, Professor?'

'Certainly not. Think about it and let me know in a day or so. In the meantime I have several letters, if

45

you would be good enough? By this evening, if you can manage that?'

'Yes, of course. Are they to go to the consultants' room or to the Medical Wing?'

'Men's Medical, please.' He bade her a placid good afternoon and went away, leaving her to tidy up and sit doing nothing, mulling over their conversation. It might be the change she wanted: the same sort of work but different surroundings, and probably different hours. She wondered where he had his consulting rooms. She was still wondering when Miss Hudson came back, as cross as two sticks because there had been no milk pudding and her teeth were in no fit state to tackle the treacle tart. Her eyes, lighting on Charity sitting in laziness, gleamed with annoyance.

'No wonder I find myself doing more than my share of the work,' she began menacingly, 'if you sit and stare at nothing the moment my back is turned.'

She sat herself down at her own desk. 'I should never have thought . . .' she went on, to be interrupted by Charity, a kind-hearted girl, not easily put out.

'Don't worry, I'll catch up,' she assured her companion, and then, 'Do I annoy you very much, Miss Hudson?'

'Indeed you do—I dare say you're a very nice girl, Charity, but you're so alive; just as though at any moment you might spring from your chair and go rushing off on an energetic ten-mile tramp. Very unsettling and most unsuitable.'

Which remark made up Charity's mind for her. She was aware that she had already made it up anyway; she liked Professor Wyllie-Lyon and a different job might be the answer to her feelings of unsettlement.

True to form Miss Hudson left on the stroke of five o'clock, leaving Charity to tidy the office and her own person, collect up the professor's papers and lock the door behind her. After an afternoon of contemplating a new job, it was disappointing to find no sign of him on Men's Medical.

Sister was there, eyeing her with suspicion, and took the letters from her with an, 'I'll see that Professor Wyllie-Lyon gets these, Miss Graham.' She added, as a cold dismissal, 'Good night.'

Charity made her way out of the hospital feeling deflated. It had been silly of her to imagine that he would be waiting for her reply. After all, what was a secretary to a man such as he? A mere cog in the wheel of his learned life.

She wished Symes good night and flounced through the door, straight into the professor's waistcoat.

'Ah, yes—where could we go that we may discuss this job?' he wanted to know.

'You said a day or two . . .'

'I find that I have to go away for a short time; I should prefer to have it all nicely settled before then.' He glanced at his watch. 'It is rather early to dine. If I might call for you at half-past seven? We could have a meal and discuss the small print.'

'Did I say that I'd take the job?' asked Charity, bemused.

'Er—no.' His smile was so friendly that she smiled back at him.

'But I feel that you are so suitable and since you are contemplating a change . . .'

He sounded so matter-of-fact about it that she found herself agreeing. 'Well, yes—I said—that is, I'd like to change jobs.'

'Splendid.' He looked down at her with an impersonal kindness which she found curiously comforting. 'Half-past seven, then?'

He stood back as she nodded and went past him, and he in his turn went into the hospital.

It was necessary to tell Aunt Emily that she was going out to dinner; that lady received the news with a naïve delight which made Charity grit her teeth. 'Just to discuss something,' she pointed out and then wished she hadn't because she had to explain about the offer of a job.

Her aunt heard her out. A new job was unimportant compared with the prospect of dining out with the professor. 'Wear something pretty,' she begged. 'The blue crêpe you bought to go out with Sidney . . .' She paused, unhappily aware that her remark hadn't been very tactful.

Charity munched a stick of celery from the dish on the kitchen table. She had no intention of wearing the blue; it reminded her of Sidney; she had bought it to please him and she had never liked it overmuch.

'I'll go and change,' she told her aunt and went up to her room to go through her wardrobe. The blue crêpe was ignored. In fact she made a mental note to give it away to Oxfam at the soonest possible opportunity, but that didn't leave much choice: last year's moss crêpe in a pleasing shade of mushroom pink or a patterned silk, perhaps a bit too colourful for a would-be aspirant for a job. She got into the crêpe. Anyone who knew anything about fashion would know that it was out-of-date, but she didn't think that Professor Wyllie-Lyon was such a person; he was far too engrossed in his work. She pinned her hair very neatly, did her face without fussing unduly, found the thin wool coat she wore to church on Sundays and, after a moment's hesitation, got into high-heeled court shoes. They had been an extravagance bought instead of the sensible pair she had intended buying; she had

had almost no chance to wear them since the one occasion she had been to the cinema with Sidney and he had expressed a restrained disapproval, commenting that they must have cost a great deal of money—which they had—and she would never get the wear out of them; she could have had two pairs of more appropriate footwear, no doubt.

'But I wanted these,' she had protested. 'They're quite beautiful and blissfully soft. It's like walking on air.'

'Probably all they are fit for,' Sidney had commented.

She eyed them with deep satisfaction now; luckily her best handbag matched well enough—and at least it was leather. She took a final look at herself in the wardrobe mirror and went down.

The professor had said half-past seven; it was five minutes after that hour. Her room was at the back of the house; she never had heard the doorbell or a sound of anyone arriving. She opened the sitting room door and let out a gusty sigh. 'Oh, you're here ... I thought . . .'

He was on his feet, smiling at her, reading her thoughts so accurately that she felt foolish.

'I'm a little early. I was explaining something of the work I hope you will be doing for me.'

Cunning, thought Charity, and saw that her father and aunt were quite won over. She gave him a direct look and he said quietly, 'But only if you want to do that, Charity.'

And then, before she needed to answer, 'Shall we go?'

He took her to the Connaught Grill Room; subdued, unassuming luxury and the kind of food she thought it unlikely she would ever be invited to eat again: tiny mushrooms in a cream and wine sauce, lobster Cardinal, and finally a purée of chestnuts with whipped cream, all accompanied by a bottle of hock which, combined with the sherry she had had before they dined, added up to a delightful evening. And there was not one word about the job until the waiter set the coffee tray before her and slid discreetly away.

They had been talking easily until now; he was a restful companion, she had discovered, unaware of the ease with which he had extracted the details of her rather dull life from her. As she passed him his cup he observed, 'You may find the hours of work trying. Normally you would work from nine o'clock until half-past four, but more often or not it will be eight-thirty until heaven knows when—inconvenient, but as you are at present er, unattached, presumably that won't be too much of a stumbling block. That is taken into account when it comes to your salary.' He mentioned a sum which made her sit up very straight.

'But that is far too much—it's more than double . . .'

'You will be doing double the work at awkward times. I shall expect you to work on a Sunday if necessary and occasionally accompany me when I go on a lecture tour. Patty Whiteman, my present secretary, will no doubt give you all the details and I'll say no more until you have met her and decided for yourself.'

He passed his cup for more coffee. 'But I should like you to work for me, Charity, and I believe you would find it rewarding. You see, the reports and letters and notes you type are concerning people; they're not meaningless invoices or yours of the 4th ult., or advertising copy. They have a purpose—I try to cure my patients. I couldn't do it without teamwork, and you would be part of that team.'

He laughed a little. 'All very pompous, but it has to be said. Shall we have some more coffee?' And then, before she could say a word, 'Tell me, how much money did your bazaar make?'

She perceived that he wasn't going to discuss his offer of a job any more, and, although she was bursting with a dozen questions about it, she held her tongue. In any case, she had already decided to work for him. Even if the hours were awkward, it would be a nice change from Miss Hudson. In fact, the irregularity of the hours would be a change ... and although she hadn't had time to give it much thought, the extra money would be a gift from heaven; Aunt Emily, bless her, was getting less and less able to be economical and relied more and more on her to let her have a little something to tide her over, and even so, there would still be enough to buy some new clothes.

She became aware that he was staring at her across the table and coloured a little. 'Sorry, I was thinking— The bazaar? Oh, they did awfully well, but they needed to, with that roof to be repaired and the Christmas choir outing and the organ fund.'

'You have lived in St John's Wood all your life?'

She shook her head. 'No, we lived at Sandford Orcas—Father had a practice in Sherborne and I went to school there. When I left, Father decided to take up a partnership in the City and we moved to St John's Wood.'

'And you chose to train as a secretary?' The question was put so casually that she answered it without hesitation.

'No, I wanted to go to university and read history ...' It was on the tip of her tongue to embark on an explanation about this; she stopped herself just in time and the professor, studying her face from under heavy lids, asked no more questions, merely remarked that for his part he was delighted at the prospect of getting a first-class secretary.

He drove her home presently, maintaining a steady flow of trivialities until they reached her door. He took the key from her and unlocked it and held it open for her to go in and only then did he say, 'If I arrange things at Augustine's, so that you are free for an hour or two tomorrow afternoon, perhaps you would like to meet my secretary? She will be able to give you a far truer picture of the work than I can. My consulting rooms are in Wigmore Street; I'll let you have the address—take a taxi there. I have a teaching round, otherwise I would drive you there myself.'

She agreed quietly. 'I'd like to see what the work is, before I decide.' She looked up into his placid face. 'Well, I have decided, really. I'd like to work for you, if you are sure that I'll do.'

She turned to go through the door. 'And thank you for a lovely evening.'

'My pleasure, Charity. And you will do, I can assure you.'

Half-way through the following morning the phone, which had rung incessantly, rang again. Miss Hudson answered it, her face thunderous as she listened. She muttered snappily into it and slammed down the receiver.

'I don't know what the world is coming to!' she declared. 'That was the office; you are to have two hours off, if you please, to undertake work for Professor Wyllie-Lyon. Whatever next, I should like to know? Well, you'll just have to stay late—I've no intention of doing any more than my normal amount.' She shot a spiteful look at Charity. 'What are you going to do, anyway?'

'Some work for Professor Wyllie-Lyon, Miss Hudson. At what time am I to go?'

'After your dinner. And if you're not back by five o'clock I shall lock up.'

Charity, who had been the last to leave for months and was always left to lock up, agreed placidly. Miss Hudson was in quite a nasty temper and there was no point in stirring a muddy pool.

Miss Hudson sniffed and maintained an injured silence until she went to her dinner, which meant that Charity could get on with her work. That suited her nicely; she had no hope of finishing before she went to her dinner and probably she wouldn't be back before five o'clock; she would have to stay and finish before she went home. She slid more paper into her machine and started on the next report.

She didn't waste time in the canteen, she gobbled down a sandwich, drank a cup of coffee and went in search of a taxi, no easy task in that part of London. All the same, it wasn't quite two o'clock as she rang the beautifully polished brass bell at the address given her by the office. The door opened automatically and she entered a discreetly carpeted hall with doors leading from it and a narrow staircase at the end. She had to scrutinise three doors before she found the professor's nameplate, as highly polished as the doorbell. Did one just walk in, she wondered, or knock and wait? She compromised—knocked and went in without waiting for an answer.

A waiting room, empty, well-furnished, with a vase or two of flowers and up-to-date magazines lying around. Very soothing, Charity thought as a door opened and a girl poked her head round it.

'Oh, good—I thought it might be you,' she said cheerfully. 'I was told to expect you about now.' She advanced into the room; a pretty girl, wearing a dress Charity instantly wanted. She was exquisitely made up, too, with her hair arranged in an artless style which must have taken ages to achieve. She held out a hand. 'I'm Patty . . .'

Charity smiled happily. She had imagined a paragon with horn-rimmed spectacles and sensible shoes. 'Charity Graham. Can you really spare me the time to show me around?'

'No appointments—the one afternoon in my working week when I'm left to catch up on everything. Shall we have a cup of coffee? Then I'll show you round and explain the work, though I don't suppose it's much different to the hospital.'

She led the way through the door into a small office carpeted in dark grey, the walls papered in a pale apricot, with the desk under the window and a padded chair behind it. A nice change from the austere office at Augustine's.

'The coffee is here,' explained Patty and opened another door, revealing a fair-sized cloakroom fitted with shelves on which were cups and saucers and glasses. There was an electric kettle and a coffee percolator and a minute refrigerator, too.

Patty got cups and saucers and poured the coffee. 'The loo's through there.' She nodded towards another door. 'Let's go back to my office, shall we?' And, once they were settled, 'Now, where shall I start . . .'

She knew her job; what was more, she enjoyed it. 'If I wasn't getting married I'd stay for ever,' she told Charity. 'All go, you know, but the professor's a dream to work for. Mind you, if he gets the bit between his teeth about some patient or other, you'll be typing reports until all hours, phoning all round the clock and acting as a kind of buffer between him and anyone getting in his way.' She was pulling open drawers in filing cabinets, explaining the intercom, opening cupboard doors to show their neatly arranged contents. 'There is a nurse, of course, who deals with patients, but you make the appointments. Do you mind travelling? He will sometimes want you to go if he is lecturing . . .'

'Where?'

'Oh, all over the place—Brussels and the Hague and Vienna and the States.'

Charity blinked. 'He didn't mention . . .'

'Forgot. He does have a lot on his mind. You'll get a cheque each month on the first; he likes to have a list of any expenses two days before that. Leave it on his desk.'

'Oh, will I have any?'

'Rather—taxis, buses, overtime. Now, come and see the consulting room.'

It was as well furnished as the waiting room, with a very large desk across one corner, crammed tidily with papers, folders, a blotter and a stationery rack. There was a curtained-off recess used as an examination room and an imitation log fire, the gas flickering cheerfully. A pleasant room and very reassuring for the patient, thought Charity, and pictured Professor Wyllie-Lyon sitting there, sympathetically listening to whoever was consulting him. She felt a thrill of excitement when she remembered that she would be sitting in the room next door.

'Well, do you think you'd like it?' asked Patty.

Charity nodded. 'Oh, yes. Do you suppose I could manage?'

'Of course you can. Anyway, Professor Wyllie-Lyon wouldn't have offered you the job if he hadn't been sure you could cope. It'll make a nice change from Augustine's. Your lunchtime may be a bit erratic, by the way; if it's a busy morning you may be a bit late; on the other hand, if the professor's at the hospital or away on a consultation, do as you please. The nurse is a sweetie—Mrs Kemp—middle-aged and cosy—been here for years. There is the porter too, Harry; he comes to clear rubbish and bring the milk and run errands and so on. The professor lives close by—he quite often walks round. He's got a house, one of those discreet Regency places with a housekeeper and a butler. Very posh. Heaps of friends, but hardly what you'd call a party man. There's a rumour going round that he's on the brink of getting engaged. I've never seen her but Mrs Kemp has; says she is a haughty piece.'

They wandered back to the tiny kitchen and Patty put the kettle on. 'Have a cup of tea before you go. I'm leaving in four-and-a-half weeks' time and Professor Wyllie-Lyon thought it might be a good idea if you worked with me for a day or two before I go. Could you manage that?'

'Yes, I am sure I can. I'll give in my notice tomorrow morning so that I can leave in a month, and come here for the last half week. Would that do?'

'Super. Do you have to go back to Augustine's now?'

Charity thought of the unfinished work on her desk. 'Yes, I'll have to work late . . .'

They perched side by side on the table, sipping their tea. 'Isn't there anyone to give a helping hand?'

'Well, there is Miss Hudson, but she likes to go at five o'clock sharp. I don't mind.'

'Got a boyfriend?'

She shook her head. 'No—not any more . . .'

Patty nodded her head vigorously. 'You have to be so sure, don't you?' She heaved a contented sigh. 'I'm sure about my George. You must come to our wedding; the professor and Mrs Kemp are coming, so you won't feel lonely.'

'I'd love to. Is it to be near here?'

'Primrose Hill in just over two months' time, so that we can be settled in by Christmas. The professor gave us a marvellous present—a combined dinner and tea and breakfast service—china, my dear, and it must have cost a bomb!'

They spent another five minutes or so on the interesting topic of wedding dresses before Charity got reluctantly to her feet. 'I'm sure that I'm going to like being here,' she said. 'I can't wait to start.'

They parted on the best of terms and she walked to the corner and got on a bus; it took longer than a taxi but she had a lot to think about. Besides, she would have to work late anyway and another twenty minutes or so wouldn't make all that difference.

It was after half past four by the time she opened the office door to find Miss Hudson seething with impatience and bad temper. 'There you are!' she exclaimed crossly. 'All this while . . . and left me to cope with all this work.'

As far as Charity could see, the work she had left on her own desk was still there and there was very little left to do on Miss Hudson's.

'Never mind,' she said kindly. 'It's almost five o'clock and you've all but finished.'

'I had to make the tea,' complained Miss Hudson, still seething.

Charity was typing briskly. 'Yes, well I expect you had to,' she observed, her mind on other things. 'I've had mine.'

She whisked an X-Ray report from the machine, inserted a sheet of paper and typed out her notice, then put it into an envelope and sealed it ready for the morning. She was aware that Miss Hudson was watching her, but she rattled away at the next report without saying a word and at five o'clock Miss Hudson, deeply suspicious, took herself smartly off home.

It was an hour later before Charity had finished, and it was quite dark as she left the hospital. The rush hour had dwindled to a steady trickle and the bus queue wasn't long. She dismissed the childish wish that Professor Wyllie-Lyon would come along in his car and give her a lift, and climbed aboard her bus to stand squashed between two bowler-hatted gentlemen with sharp elbows. Not that she noticed; she had too much to occupy her thoughts.

She told her father and aunt that evening and was a little surprised to find them so enthusiastic. Her job at the hospital was sure and steady and there was always the chance that she and the professor might end up at odds with each other.

'You can take a little holiday before you start, dear,' said Aunt Emily.

Charity explained that she planned to go to her new job the day after she left Augustine's. 'And the hours may be a bit erratic, although I understand that they are made up to me. I don't mind that a bit, it'll make a nice change from nine till five and knowing exactly what work I'm going to do. I may have to accompany Professor Wyllie-Lyon when he goes to a seminar or does a lecture tour.'

Aunt Emily, still living by the standards of her own youth, frowned a little but her father observed, 'Splendid. You may see something of the world, and meet people. I was only thinking, my dear, that our own circle of friends is a narrow one and you have little opportunity of meeting fresh faces.'

A speech which surprised Charity very much indeed.

She saw nothing of the professor for several days, although she received a letter confirming her appointment as his secretary. When she did see him, he was standing in the entrance hall, talking to two of the honorary consultants and, although he smiled and nodded to her as she went past, he made no attempt to speak. She felt vaguely disappointed for no particular reason, but in any case she hadn't the leisure to worry about it; Miss Hudson, apprised of her departure, was intent on getting the last ounce of work out of her before she left. Another girl was taking her place but, as Miss Hudson said darkly, she might be unreliable and she, Miss Hudson, still had a string of appointments with her dentist which necessitated her leaving early at least twice a week. Charity, who had had the task of showing her successor round, thought it likely that Miss Hudson might have to change the times of the dental appointments, for the new assistant had stated quite clearly and in no uncertain terms that she intended working her hours and no more than that. Charity felt quite sorry for Miss Hudson, even when she was working late in order to clear up the very large half of their work which that lady decided was her share.

It was half-way through the month before she saw the professor to speak to. She had heard in the canteen that he had been away on a lecture tour, but she didn't know that he was back until he walked into the office while Miss Hudson was at her dinner.

He handed Charity a bundle of papers, at the same

time wishing her good afternoon and expressing the hope that she could have them ready by five o'clock.

Having done this he showed no wish to leave. He sat down on Miss Hudson's desk and looked her over thoughtfully. 'You and Patty discussed the job?'

'Yes, we did,' said Charity matter-of-factly. 'Didn't she tell you? I'm looking forward to starting, only I'm a bit scared, too.'

'Don't be, I don't bite. You do understand that you will be more or less your own boss? You'll have to work like a Trojan, but you can arrange things to suit yourself, as long as the work is done. And if at the end of a month you feel that you just can't work like that, tell me.'

'I think I can cope, Professor Wyllie-Lyon.' She waved a well-shaped, capable hand. 'The office alone is enough to spur me on, after this . . .'

He laughed and the door opened and Miss Hudson came in. She hadn't enjoyed her dinner—mince and carrots, and she disliked both—and the sight of two people laughing so easily together caused her to look sourly at Charity, even while she wished the professor a grudging good afternoon.

'Women's Surgical wants that report on Mrs Evans before two o'clock,' she said and turned back to the professor. 'We're kept busy, sir, as you can see; I sometimes wonder how I keep going and now I hear that Charity is to work for you, so that I must miss what little help I get from her . . .'

He said smoothly, 'Perhaps you have no need of assistance, Miss Hudson? The administration are always looking for ways and means of cutting down the runnings costs. I'm sure that they would be only too glad . . .'

Miss Hudson's tongue tripped over itself in her

haste to deny this. 'No, no, sir. There is a great deal of routine work which I haven't the time for. I'm sure that I shall miss Charity.'

The professor wandered to the door. 'Your loss is my gain, Miss Hudson.'

A remark which buoyed Charity up for the remainder of the month.

She spent the last day showing the new girl the ropes. There was already something of an atmosphere between her and Miss Hudson; Charity wondered how long it would be before they fell out and then remembered happily that it didn't concern her any more.

She arrived early at her new job, with Patty hard on her heels. The phone rang as they went into the office: the professor, to say that he had been at the hospital during the night and had only just got home.

'I'll be half an hour,' he told Patty. 'Do the apologising, will you, and have the coffee on the boil.'

She relayed this to Charity, adding casually, 'This happens from time to time. We soothe any patients waiting and hand out magazines and small talk. He said half an hour, so it will be just that. Be an angel and put on the kettle while I do my hair, then we'll go into the waiting room. Mrs Kemp will be here soon and she'll take over while we get the notes ready.'

There were five patients with appointments. 'Half an hour each,' said Patty, 'give or take five minutes; that gives him time to have coffee before he goes to Augustine's—he is due there at midday. There are three patients for the afternoon, starting at three o'clock, but he'll be back before then, dictating or whatever. You'll get most of it typed by five o'clock

but sometimes there is the odd patient in the evening.'
She grinned at Charity. 'Play it by ear, love.'

But it wasn't as bad as it sounded; Professor Wyllie-
Lyon sat himself down behind his desk exactly on
time, bade them both good morning, expressed the
wish that Charity would be happy in her work and
asked if he might have a cup of coffee when he had
seen his first patient.

He handed over his post to be dealt with, studied
the notes before him and pressed the buzzer on his
desk as the two of them went back to the office, where
they sorted the post, put the bills on one side,
consigned the advertisements to the waste-paper
basket and saw to the coffee.

Charity took it in, 'For you might as well start as
you mean to go on,' said Patty. 'Bring out the notes of
the first patient—he'll have scribbled instructions on
them.'

He was sitting back with his eyes shut as she went
in. He looked tired to the bone, but only for a
moment. He sat up at once, looking as he always did,
calm and unworried and even-tempered. He looked
immaculate, too, just as though he'd had a long night's
sleep and all the time in the world in which to dress
and eat his breakfast.

He nodded his thanks, handed her the notes and
pulled the next folder towards him and she went back
to Patty, waiting with two mugs of coffee.

'Mrs Kemp has hers when he is finished; she'd
rather. What's he written?'

Appointments for X-Ray and the Path. Lab; the
patient to be seen again in two weeks; letter to her own
doctor. Charity was left to deal with these and the
succeeding four and when the last patient had gone
she went in with her notebook and took down letters.

She was glad that her shorthand was good, for he went fast and he didn't hesitate.

'I'd like those after lunch,' he said. 'You two girls arrange your lunchtime between you; I'll be back at two o'clock.'

He had spoken pleasantly but briskly so that she didn't feel encouraged to say anything at all beyond a polite, 'Yes, sir,' as he went away.

She took her notebook back and began on the letters, while Patty got out the afternoon's notes and decided to go out to lunch. 'You'll be just about ready by the time I get back. It's a chance for you to see if you can get that little lot done for him.'

She was back in less than an hour, and Charity, surveying the neat pile waiting for signature, asked, 'Where do I go? Is there somewhere close by?'

'There is a little coffee shop five minutes walk away. Turn left and then left again. You can eat here if you want to. I do when the weather is bad. When you are on your own you will have to arrange it with Mrs Kemp—she's no trouble though—she'll go to lunch first or last; it's according to how many patients there are and how much work you have got.' She added encouragingly, 'It's a nice quiet day, today.'

'Well, let's hope that there isn't a busy one until I've got dug in,' said Charity and went off in search of a sandwich and coffee.

She took more dictation until three o'clock and found a small pile of letters on her desk, as well, with cryptic notes scrawled on them. Mostly invitations with 'refuse' written over them. Not very sociably minded, Charity decided, tapping away as though her life depended on it.

She missed Patty when she left, two days later, but by then she was fairly confident that she could manage the work. She liked Mrs Kemp; the two of them got on well together. She also liked the work, so much more interesting than it had been at Augustine's; besides, there was no Miss Hudson . . .

Patty had been gone a week when what Mrs Kemp called, 'A day to get your teeth into, dear,' occurred. Charity was putting the cover on her machine as the clock struck six, glad that the day was over, when the professor came into the office. That he was annoyed she could see at once, for his face was expressionless. He handed her a fistful of reports, with the request that he might have them within half an hour.

'Miss Hudson and the new girl have fallen out,' he observed, 'so that each of them do as little work as they possibly can. There was no hope of getting these done at Augustine's and I need them first thing in the morning.'

Charity took the cover off her typewriter again and got forms from the drawer in her desk. There weren't many, six or seven, but she was already late. She had started on the first one when he said: 'I'm sorry—you're late already. Leave them and go home.'

'Half an hour's work,' she assured him, and started on the second.

She was prevented from going on with it by his hand coming down on hers. 'No, go home, Charity. You can do them in the morning as soon as you get here.' He took his hand away and crossed the room to his own door.

'Good night.'

The tone of his voice didn't allow for dispute. She tidied up once more, put on her outdoor things, called a good night and went to the front door. It was dark and raining and she paused, considering which was the quickest way to the bus stop. She was about to close the door behind her when she heard a hesitant tapping. She listened for the next few moments and then closed the door again and went back to the professor's door. The light was out in the waiting room, but the door to her office was half open. He was sitting at her desk, looking quite out of place, his large person bent over her typewriter, quite absorbed, thumping away with two fingers.

CHAPTER FOUR

CHARITY cast off her coat and flung her gloves and handbag after it. 'Now, now!' she said chidingly. 'This won't do! You don't keep a dog and bark yourself!' She had quite forgotten who he was for the moment.

She remembered when he glanced up at her. 'I told you to go home, Charity.'

'Oh, dear, I didn't mean to be rude; I'm sorry; but that's my work, sir. I expected to work late sometimes you know—Patty did tell me that; so did you. If, however, you wouldn't mind getting up . . .?'

He had been looking at her with an expressionless face; now suddenly he smiled. 'Very well, Charity, on one condition—that I drive you home. I've some phone calls to make; probably you will be finished by then?'

She was covering her typewriter again when he came out of his room and closed the door. He signed the forms, put them into his case and waited while she switched off the lights and locked the doors. Charity, being helped into her coat, thought what nice manners he had, and when she saw the rain teeming down, felt relief that he had offered to drive her home.

He didn't talk much during the short drive and she was content to sit beside him in an unspoken friendliness which she had begun to think had been lost between them. At her door she asked him diffidently if he would like to go in.

'Yes I would,' he told her, 'but unfortunately I've a dinner engagement.'

'Well, thank you for giving me a lift, sir.' He had got out with her and was holding the gate open. 'Good night.'

She went into the house without looking round and stood listening to the gentle purr of the car as he drove away. He would be spending the evening with the girl he was going to marry, no doubt. Very beautiful, Mrs Kemp had said; very haughty, too. A most unsuitable wife for the professor, she had said. She had glanced at Charity as she had said it. 'There's plenty of girls just as lovely and far more suitable.'

The professor was going away at the end of the week: a lecturing tour in Canada. He would be gone for a week and, although she would be going to his consulting rooms each day, there wouldn't be much to do. His letters she was to deal with as she thought fit, and he had told her when she might make appointments. He had also left her an article which he had written for the *Lancet*; she was to check it for punctuation and type it for him.

Mrs Kemp was having a week's holiday and Charity found it a little lonely, even though she enjoyed working as she pleased. Half-way through the week the professor telephoned, his voice very clear from all those miles away. She had been so pleased to hear him that she hadn't said a word until he asked her if anything was the matter.

'No, oh, no!' said Charity. 'It's just such a nice surprise. There are some letters I don't know how to answer.'

'Read them.'

Which she duly did, making hasty notes on each.

'Nothing else? Good. Charity, take the keys for my desk and unlock the centre drawer; there are two tapes there. Type them for me, please. I shall be back this

weekend and will see you on Monday morning.' He
said goodbye and hung up.

She answered the letters first and then went and got
the tapes. They were a long involved series of lecture
notes which kept her busy for the rest of that day and
a good deal of the next, too.

She was glad when the weekend was over, she felt
impatient of the gentle routine at home. The weather
had turned cold and wet and there was little to do in
the garden. She cooked the meals, made an attractive
audience while her father enthused over an eighteenth-
century grammar he had discovered in a dusty
bookshop in some forgotten alley behind Fleet Street,
and went to church, all the while aware that it wasn't
enough to content her any more. She was uncertain as
to why this was but it certainly got her up early on
Monday morning, and she was half an hour early at
Wigmore Street.

Mrs Kemp wasn't due for another thirty minutes and
the first patients wouldn't arrive until mid-morning.
Charity picked up the milk bottle from the doorstep,
unlocked the front door and went along to Professor
Wyllie-Lyon's door, unlocked that and went in. The
waiting room was dim and rather chilly; she pulled the
curtains back as she went, and opened her office door.
The door between it and the professor's room was
open and she stopped short at the sight of him sitting
at his desk, writing.

He glanced up and smiled. 'Good morning, Charity.
Make some coffee will you? I've dealt with the stuff
you left for me; there'll be plenty more for you to type
presently.'

'Good morning, sir. When did you get in? Oughtn't
you to have breakfast?' She managed to keep her voice
matter-of-fact.

'I had that on board—we got in at six o'clock—it seemed pointless to go to bed. I'll go home and shower and shave and get back here in time for the first patient. Mrs Caldwell, isn't it?'

She had put on the kettle, and milk in a saucepan to heat. 'Yes, at ten-thirty. She rang to make sure you'd be here.'

She took the cover off her typewriter and readied her desk for the morning's work, feeling happy. 'She sounded worried.'

'She has lymphadenoma—do you know what that is?'

'I looked it up in the medical directory. It's terminal, isn't it?'

He had left his desk and was leaning in the doorway between the two rooms, watching her as she made the coffee. 'Yes, but with care we'll be able to keep her alive for some time yet, and when it gets beyond my powers I'll pass her on to the surgeons.'

'Do you ever give up?' asked Charity.

'No, never.' He came to take his mug from her. 'And that doesn't apply only to medicine.' He sat astride the other chair by her desk. 'No worries during the week?'

She shook her head. 'No, thank you. I've made a lot of appointments for you: they are in your diary on the desk.'

'I've seen them, thank you. You don't miss Augustine's?'

'Heavens, no. I'm very happy here and I like the work. You're quite satisfied with me, sir?' She hadn't meant to ask, but she had to know.

'Quite satisfied, Charity. You're coping very well, just as I expected you to. A good thing, for I have a number of meetings and a lecture or two during the next few weeks...' He was interrupted by the telephone ringing and Charity answered it.

A woman's voice, high and imperious. 'Is Professor Wyllie-Lyon there yet? If he is, tell him it's Brenda. I want to speak to him, it's urgent.'

Charity handed him the receiver. 'A lady called Brenda; she says it's urgent.'

She went into the cloakroom and shut the door, trying not to hear the murmur of his voice. It was a lengthy conversation and, judging by the frown on his face when he had finished and she had gone back to her office, an unsatisfactory one. He had gone back to his own room but presently he returned with a folder of papers for her to deal with.

'Will you stay on this evening?' he wanted to know. 'I'll dictate as much as I can before the afternoon patients, but there is an appointment I must keep at six o'clock. I should be back here by seven o'clock and that will mean another hour or so's work for you. I'm sorry, Charity, it's something I promised...'

She answered calmly, 'That's quite all right, sir, I'm not doing anything this evening, anyway.'

He turned away. 'Well, you should be. You should be out dancing every night with a string of young men after you.'

She was too surprised to answer that. She watched him close the door quietly behind him and then, since there was nothing to be learned from its smooth mahogany surface, she applied herself to the task of assembling the notes of the morning patients.

He went away presently, leaving her to brood over the telephone call. It had annoyed him and yet he had agreed to whatever the caller had wanted, even though it meant disrupting his evening—hers, too, although of course she was paid for that. This perhaps was the girl he was going to marry. She gathered up the notes and took them through to his desk, where she arranged them just so, making sure that everything was just as he liked it. There was something on it which hadn't been there before: a large framed photo of a girl—Charity looked closer—no, a woman, very attractive, well dressed, smiling at the camera from an exquisitely made-up face. 'Every day of thirty,' said Charity, studying the face carefully. Handsome, she conceded, and nothing soft about its owner; the kind of woman who would be a splendid hostess, run her house without effort and take no interest in her children; sticky fingers and eggy mouths just wouldn't be in her line of country. Charity went back to her desk and got on with her work; Mrs Kemp would be arriving at any moment now and she would want a little gossip after her week's holiday. Charity got up again and put on the kettle.

She had several letters ready for the professor to sign by the time he returned and she finished the rest between furnishing him with the patients' notes and collecting those that he'd finished with, so that her desk, and his, were clear by the time he left for the hospital. She left Mrs Kemp to tidy her examination room and went along to the coffee shop for her lunch, taking the precaution of buying herself a packet of sandwiches at the same time; the day was going to be a long one. It reminded her that she must ring her aunt and tell her that she would be home late.

There were several jobs to be done when she got back. Mrs Kemp went for her own lunch, and Charity did some filing, opened the second post and sharpened her pencil.

It was half past four before the last patient was ushered out. Chairty had prudently made tea and had her own before she took a cup in to the professor. He took it absent-mindedly, merely saying, 'Bring your notebook in, Charity.' He looked tired now, and remote.

She sat down quietly while he dictated his letters and requests for X-Rays, barium meals and the like, and then took herself off to her own room and started work on them. There was enough to keep her busy for more than an hour and there was more to come, he had said. He opened her door presently. 'I'll be back by seven o'clock.' He smiled briefly as he went.

She had eaten her sandwich and had a cup of tea, finished her typing and was tidying a cupboard when he came back, exactly when he had said he would. He had changed into another suit and it was richly sombre. He looked handsome, assured and most beautifully turned out, but he also looked tired and, judging by the blandness of his face, was hiding annoyance; but he asked her if she had had something to eat before he sat down to dictate.

He went fast as he was wont to do, but she was used to that now and there were only four letters and a couple of reports. She closed her notebook and started for the door.

'I'll wait and sign them,' he told her. 'I've some work to do . . .'

The phone rang as she began to type and the same haughty voice demanded to speak to him. Charity switched on the intercom and switched the call through to his office. She longed to eavesdrop; it was a long phone call.

She offered to make him coffee when she had finished and taken the letters through for him to sign, but he refused in an absent-minded manner which betrayed the fact that his mind was elsewhere so she bade him good night and went to get her coat. He was waiting for her in her office and at her look of surprise he said, 'I've kept you very late; the most I can do is to see you home.'

'There's no need, there's a bus . . .'

'I am aware of that; I shall take you home.' His tone was pleasant, remote and final; all the same she had another try.

'When I took this job, professor, you told me that I would sometimes work late and I accepted that. You can't keep taking me home like this.'

He opened the door. 'You talk too much,' he told her gently.

Outside her door she hesitated. He had got out and had opened the car door and she stood on the pavement, trying to make up her mind.

'If you are wondering whether to ask me in for a cup of coffee, I shall be delighted to do so,' he said blandly and then chuckled at her startled look.

It hadn't been just coffee, reflected Charity, presently curled up in bed. It had been sandwiches and a plate of mince pies her aunt had made that afternoon and whisky with her father in the study afterwards while they had continued an absorbing discussion on Thomas Carlyle's works. Charity, sitting with Aunt Emily, listening with half an ear to an account of that lady's shopping expedition in search of a pair of stout shoes, could hear the occasional rumble of laughter and murmur of voices. She went to bed presently, saying rather huffily that she had to go to work in the morning.

'A delightful evening,' her father commented at breakfast. 'He's an Oxford man, of course—went to Magdalen—years after my time, of course. Looked him up—brilliant man—rugger player, too—past it now.'

'He's not old, Father.' Charity spoke rather more fiercely than she had meant to.

'Old? Of course not, my dear. Five-and-thirty—but his work doesn't allow him to turn out for a regular game.' Mr Graham, not an observant man, cast an enquiring eye towards his daughter and then went on with his breakfast.

Professor Wyllie-Lyon was going to Augustine's first in the morning; the patients were not booked until eleven o'clock. Charity had the place to herself until Mrs Kemp arrived at around ten o'clock and they had their coffee together before going about their separate jobs. Exactly on the hour she heard the waiting room door open and a moment later her own door was opened. The professor came in, but not alone. The man with him was younger than he; dark curly hair, light blue eyes, of middle height and with a pleasant, good-natured face.

The professor said good morning and went on, 'This is Dr Kemble, from New Zealand—over here to pick up some ideas about leukemia. He is seconded to Augustine's for a short time. There are some old case histories he would like to borrow. Turn them up for me, will you, Charity? They'll be filed in that end cabinet.' He added a short list of names. 'Let me know if you can't find them.'

He nodded briefly and closed the door behind him, leaving Charity and Dr Kemble together.

'Sit down,' she invited. 'It may take a minute or two, I'm fairly new here.'

He looked around him. 'Plenty to do, I dare say? Professor Wyllie-Lyon's a busy man, so I'm told. Top of the tree, isn't he?'

She wasn't sure if one doctor should talk of another in that fashion; perhaps they had different ideas in New Zealand. She said cautiously. 'He's well known . . .'

He was quick. 'Ah, shouldn't say things like that to his secretary, I dare say. Don't hold it against me. I'm a great admirer of his work; hope I'll be half as good.'

She rather liked him. 'I'm sure you will, Dr Kemble. Here are the case histories; are you going to take them with you?'

'Please. You want me to sign for them?' He lingered on his way to the door. 'Am I going too fast if I ask you to have dinner with me this evening?'

'Much too fast, Dr Kemble.' But she smiled at him as she said it. He would ask her again, she was sure of that, and then she would say yes. At the same time there was a half-hidden regret that it couldn't be Professor Wyllie-Lyon who wanted to take her out. But of course there was the beauty whose photo had pride of place on his desk; he would have no eyes for other women.

She got on with her morning's work, the epitome of the perfect secretary: making appointments, finding notes, producing coffee for a patient who had mild hysterics when the professor told her, in the most guarded terms, that she had a heart murmur. His manner towards the lady was faultless, but Charity sensed his impatience at her goings-on; after all, he dealt with out-patients by the dozen in his out-patient department at St Augustine's, most of them stoically prepared to make the best of it under his guidance, and equally determined to carry on with whatever job they were doing. Mrs Kemp bore the lady away finally and the professor, without saying a word over and above his instructions as to treatment, dismissed

Charity with a nod and rang the bell for his next patient.

By the end of the day she had decided that something was on his mind; behind the façade of placid calm he was worried. No, she corrected herself, not worried; occupied with a problem. 'Not that it's any business of mine,' she told the empty rooms as she prepared to go home, the last to leave. And hard on that thought, the astonishing one that it was her business, her own private business; the professor's happiness was something quite vital to her. She wanted him to be happy above all things for she loved him more than anything or anyone else in the world. 'And of all the silly things to do,' she exclaimed crossly, 'that's just about the silliest.'

She paused in her tidying of her desk and sat down to think about it. She was in love; it was exciting and delightful and utterly hopeless. Even if there hadn't been the beauty on his desk, he was hardly likely to look at her with anything more than appreciation of her capabilities.

She got up and fetched her coat, locked the doors and left. But instead of going to the bus stop, her feet, obeying her unconscious wish, bore her out of Wigmore Street and into the quiet backwater where he lived. The houses here were terraced, tall elegant residences built during the Regency, skilfully modernised and expensively maintained. There were no front gardens, only elegant iron railings and discreetly curtained windows and front doors with elaborate pediments. The professor's house was the last in the short terrace, with an arched entrance beside it leading, she supposed, to mews garages at the back. There were lights in the downstairs windows and shining through the fanlight over the front door, and she crossed the narrow street to observe it more clearly from the opposite side.

As well she did and that she was standing in the shadow, away from the lamp posts, for the street door opened and he came out, leaving the door open behind him, turning under the arch, no doubt to fetch his car. There wouldn't be time to get to the end of the street before the car lights picked her out; she opened the wrought iron gate leading to the area of the house behind her, and stepped silently half-way down its steps.

She was mad, she told herself, standing there in the cold of a December evening, and nothing like this was ever going to happen again. She went down a couple of steps as the Bentley slid from under the archway and its lights picked up everything in their beam, but since the car had stopped outside his house, she felt emboldened to peep through the railings. The door was still open and coming through it was the woman in the photograph; even at that distance Charity could see that she was handsome, wrapped in a fur coat, fair hair shining in the lights from the house. She could hear her voice, too, high and impatient, complaining about something. The professor had got out of the car and was waiting by its open door, and if he spoke it was so softly that she couldn't hear him as he helped his companion in and got in himself and presently drove away.

'So now you know,' muttered Charity to herself, hurrying to catch her bus. She spent a miserable night; she had had no idea that being in love could be so unsettling. She had imagined herself in love half a dozen times, and there had been Sidney, of course, but with hindsight she knew now that none of these tepid affairs had been more than skin deep, and she knew just as surely that, however hard she tried, she would never be able to summon up anything more than tepid feelings for any other man.

'You're a fool,' she told herself, her head buried in the pillows, and wept herself to sleep.

Neither her aunt nor her father were particularly observant; her aunt remarked that she looked as though she might be starting a cold and her father, without looking up from his newspaper, advised her to dose herself with something. But their remarks were in passing; her aunt was far too busy making a list of the extra groceries she would need for Christmas to do more than agree vaguely. 'It's still some time to Christmas,' she murmured, 'but you know what the shops are—barely a month and I haven't yet made the pudding.'

Puddings held no interest for Charity; she crumbled toast, drank her coffee and said that she had to get to work earlier than usual, which brought forth her aunt's remark that that nice man worked her too hard, and when was he coming to see them again? Charity couldn't think of a safe reply to this, so she kissed her companions and five minutes later left the house.

She couldn't get to Wigmore Street fast enough; just to see him again would make her day. It wasn't until she was putting the key in the door that she paused to wonder how she would feel when she did see him. Pray heaven she wouldn't blush or make a fool of herself. She was his efficient secretary, nothing more, and she must remember that from now on. It struck her then that that wasn't going to be so easy; she would have to be on her guard.

She stood before the looking-glass in the cloakroom and studied her face; it looked all right, a bit red round the eyes, but he wouldn't notice that. It was her manner towards him—she would have to be very careful.

She was so careful that when Professor Wyllie-Lyon arrived he asked her after a few minutes if she felt unwell. 'Or swallowed the poker,' he added. 'Have I done something to vex you?'

'No,' said Charity hurriedly, 'of course not. I—I have a headache.' She gave him a beseeching look, although she was unaware of that, begging him to believe her, and he turned away, apparently satisfied. 'Make yourself some tea,' he advised kindly, 'and you'd better take a couple of Panadol.'

He enquired about the headache when she went to fetch the first patient's notes, not looking at her, his head bent over his desk, and she told him that it had gone. She hadn't had one in the first place, anyway, but it had been the first excuse that she could think of.

There were no patients in the afternoon. She cleared up the outstanding work, made tea for Mrs Kemp, who was giving the examination room its weekly turn out, and herself, and left promptly.

After a day or two she found that she could cope very nicely. She hadn't known that loving someone could hurt so much, nor had she known that it was possible to hide the hurt behind a calm face. She had spent a sleepless night wondering if it would be better to leave her job, go away and never see him again, but she knew that she could never do that—half a loaf was better than no bread.

It was the following morning that Dr Kemble came again, ostensibly to return the case papers but actually to ask her to have dinner with him. This time she agreed. She had decided, after realising she loved the professor, to refuse if he should ever ask her again, but the sight of the professor sitting at his desk starring down at the lovely face smiling at him from its expensive frame had been a bad beginning to her day. Dr Kemble was pleasant and friendly and perhaps he would help her to rid her mind of the professor. She declined that evening, though; for one thing there were several patients coming during the afternoon and she might have to stay later than usual. There were only two booked for the day after and, before she went to ask the professor if he wanted to see Dr Kemble, they agreed that he should call for her the following evening.

'He might as well wait if he has nothing better to do and I'll give him a lift to Augustine's—he is doing outpatients with me this morning. Give him a cup of coffee, Charity.'

He had given her a quick smile, his glance impersonal.

Dinner with Guy Kemble turned out to be surprisingly pleasant. He was a good talker, never very serious, making her laugh a great deal. He took her to Nick's Diner because, he explained ingenuously, someone back home had told him it was a good place to go. Over their shrimp cocktails, steak tartare and crêpe Suzette, he told her something of his life in New Zealand. He was going back there, of course; there was a job waiting for him—senior registrar at the big Auckland Hospital, and hopefully a consultant's post at the end of it.

'That's why I'm here,' he explained, 'picking Professor Wyllie-Lyon's brains and learning all I can—specialising.' He added awkwardly, 'I want to make the grade—there's a girl . . .'

'She must be proud of you,' said Charity promptly. 'Don't you miss her?'

He nodded. 'I wrote and told her about you and said

I was going to ask you to go out with me. I—I like to talk about her, of course, and I thought you'd listen; I mean, you look as though you might.'

'Of course I'll listen. Tell me all about her.'

It took the rest of their meal and he was still talking as they waited on the pavement for a taxi. Neither of them saw the professor driving past alone in the Bentley. He saw them, but he didn't stop.

He was at his desk when Charity got to work in the morning, wished her good morning, asked her to make coffee and bent his head over his work again. It was when she took the coffee tray in that he looked up and asked, 'You had a pleasant evening with Guy?'

She was so surprised she almost dropped the tray. 'However did you know?' she began, and then, 'Yes, I enjoyed myself, thank you, sir.'

'Dare say you have a good deal in common.' He took the cup she offered him and sugared it.

'Well—I don't know about that.' She stood uncertainly, the tray in her hand, wondering if he wanted to talk. Apparently he did, for he said, 'Get a cup and come in here and drink it, Charity. There's no rush this morning.'

But he had nothing to say for a few minutes and she sat quietly, studying his face covertly. It was calm, as always, but the calm was a cover for something else; tiredness, or worry, or anger. She had no idea which was uppermost. She longed to say, 'Look, tell me what's wrong?' and knew that that was an impossibility.

He looked up and caught her eyes on him. 'I'm tired,' he said, just as though he were answering her unspoken question. 'Too many late nights. It's a good thing I'm off lecturing next week.'

'It's rather close to Christmas . . .'

'Just Brussels, and only for two days. There'll be a good deal of work for you when I get back.' He put down his cup and settled back in his chair. 'I'm going to Norway in the new year—ten days or so of lecturing; I'd like you to come along to share some of the workload, Charity.'

Her heart gave a great jump and rocked her ribs. 'Me?' she squeaked. 'Go with you?'

'Unless you have any real objection.' He was looking at her thoughtfully. 'It's quite usual, you know.'

She went pink. 'Oh, it's not that. It's such a heavenly surprise and I don't mind how hard I work. Do you go somewhere each day?'

'Not quite.' He was smiling at her enthusiasm. 'Travelling will take up quite some time at this time of the year. We shall fly a good deal, of course. I'll let you have the itinerary after Christmas.'

He picked up his pen and opened a folder. 'And now we had better get on with our work.'

She was at the door when he said, 'Oh, by the way, if Guy Kemble wants to take you out any time, let me know and we'll fix an early evening for you.'

There was a lot she could have said to that. 'That's very kind of you, sir,' was all she did say.

'You're only young once,' said the professor. 'He must be lonely when he is not working.'

It was on the tip of her tongue to tell him about the girl waiting for Guy, that he spent a good deal of his leisure time contentedly writing long letters to her, but it was hardly her business. She murmured something or other and went back to her office, feeling peevish. What she did in her free time was her own business and that didn't include Guy Kemble. And why was the professor taking an interest anyway?

She sighed as she settled down to work. Of course, if he had taken an interest in her—but that was wishful thinking with a vengeance; she mustn't allow her feelings to get the upper hand. She went to fetch the first patient's notes presently, her pretty face ironed into such wooden composure that his quick glance became a stare.

'You're feeling all right?' he wanted to know.

'Yes, thank you, sir.' Her voice was as wooden as her stare.

They had an uneasy relationship for the rest of the day. True, the professor's manner hadn't altered one jot; he was as pleasant and placid as he always was but he had, as it were, retired to a distance, and the distance was lengthening rapidly. If they went on like this much longer, thought Charity, they would be reduced to a cold civility. Something would have to be done, but she didn't know what. In the event, she worried unnecessarily; fate, in the shape of a large, gaunt dog, was at her elbow.

He was dragging himself down the middle of the street when she arrived at work on Monday morning. He was hurt and dazed and yelping piteously, and none of the cars avoiding him stopped; indeed, sooner or later he was going to get run over. A car, going too fast, brushed past him and he panicked and ran across the road as best he might, hampered by the stout rope trailing from his neck.

Charity went after him, holding up an imperious hand to the oncoming traffic, not heeding the squeal of brakes and the angry shouts. The dog was standing still now, swaying a little, and she was almost near enough to snatch at the rope . . .

'Don't move,' said the professor softly as he went past her, picked up the rope and went slowly up to the dog, taking no notice at all of the snarl-up of traffic around him. He picked the beast up and rejoined her, then they crossed the street together.

'If you would unlock the door?' he suggested mildly and went through to his own rooms to the cloakroom, where he laid the dog gently on the floor. Charity, hard on his heels, filled a bowl with water and put it by the dog, who lay panting quietly. The professor cast off his coat and squatted down beside him, allowed him to drink and then set about examining him.

'No bones broken, by a miracle. He's tired out and starved. Have we any food? Milk or something?'

Charity produced milk and watched the dog guzzle it down and then drop his head back on to the floor.

'There's a blanket in the cupboard. Bring it here, will you, Charity? I think the best thing is for me to carry him to my house—there's someone there who will look after him. He's been roughly treated but as far as I can see all that he needs is food and rest . . .'

'And someone to mind about him,' added Charity fiercely. 'All those hard-hearted idiots not caring—he could have been killed.'

She fetched the blanket and he said, 'Look in the phone book on my desk; under V—my vet's number is there. Ask him to go to my house, will you? What time is my first patient?'

'Nine o'clock.'

He was wrapping the dog in the blanket and she went to open the door for him. He paused when he reached it, looking down at her, a look on his face she couldn't understand. 'It's no good me telling you not to go around rescuing stray animals for I know you wouldn't listen, but don't do it too often, my heart won't stand it.'

He bent and kissed her very gently.

CHAPTER FIVE

CHARITY closed the door after him and stood leaning against it. She had been taken by surprise and she wanted to think about it. She was still there when someone outside turned the handle and tried to get in—Mrs Kemp, putting a puzzled face round the edge of the door as Charity stood up and pulled it open.

'Hallo,' said Mrs Kemp. 'Whatever are you doing here? My goodness, I thought it might be burglars or something . . .'

Charity gave her a dazzling smile. 'I came down to let Professor Wyllie-Lyon out. There was a dog in the street—a stray—and the traffic wouldn't stop. We went after it. It's all right; he's taken it to his house . . .'

Mrs Kemp studied the smile. After a little pause she said, 'Just what he would do, bless him. I suppose there's a frightful mess in his room?'

'No,' said Charity dreamily, 'in the cloakroom—I'll clear it up.'

She wandered over behind Mrs Kemp's solid back and set to work to restore order and get the coffee percolator going. She would have to get on with her work, too; she got out patients' notes and arranged the files neatly, her head full of those brief moments at the door. Just what had he meant? And he had kissed her! She hugged the glorious fact to herself. She would have liked more time to enjoy the memory, but she could hear Mrs Kemp talking in the waiting room; the first patients would have arrived.

She sat down at her desk and then jumped up again to take a look at her face in the looking-glass in the cloakroom. Her glowing, bright-eyed face stared back at her; she added a touch more lipstick, patted the little curls which had escaped from the french pleat, and went back to her desk. She had barely begun to type when the door opened and the professor walked in.

She wasn't sure what she expected, certainly not this matter-of-fact aloofness.

He said without preamble, 'He'll do—the vet's on his way; someone's cleaning the beast up—he must have been straying for a long time.' He paused at the door. 'Let me have the X-Rays for Mrs Foster, will you?'

He went into his consulting room and closed the door quietly.

Buoyed up by rage and disappointment, she was the perfect secretary. He went to Augustine's presently, came back to see his patients in the afternoon, then back to the hospital for an emergency, pausing this time long enough to tell her that the vet had phoned to say that the dog needed only care and good food to make a good recovery.

She finished her work in the silent place; Mrs Kemp had gone home. She added the last letter to the pile to be signed, covered her machine, tidied the cloakroom and put on her coat. She felt utterly dispirited. Why, oh, why, couldn't she have fallen head over heels in love with Sidney instead of this remote man who looked upon her merely as a cog in the well-oiled machinery of his daily life?

She switched out the lights and went to the door just as the professor opened it and came in. He said easily, 'Ah, there you are. If you're ready we'll have a look at that dog?'

She goggled at him. 'Dog? He's at your home . . .'

'Well, of course he is. You'd like a look at him, wouldn't you? He has had a good day, and he has to have a name too, now.'

'You'll keep him? Oh, I'm so glad. I'm sure he'll be devoted to you because you rescued him.'

'And to you, Charity—you rescued him, too.' He sat down at her desk and started to sign the letters she had put ready for him to read through in the morning. 'I'll be in late tomorrow; get these off this evening, will you?'

So she put down her bag and folded the letters into their envelopes and stamped them and put them into her bag and then preceded him out into the street. It was cold and damp and they walked briskly, saying little.

The professor let himself into his house and ushered her before him as a portly man with grey hair and several chins crossed the hall to meet them. His 'Good evening, sir,' was uttered in a nice mixture of respect and familiarity as he cast his eyes upon Charity.

'This is Miss Graham, Snook, come to see the dog.' He glanced at her. 'Snook runs this place for me with his wife. He taught me to ride a bike and to fish.'

Charity held out a hand. 'I hope the dog hasn't given you too much to do,' she observed and beamed at the man.

'Indeed no, miss. A very docile beast, if I might say so. He's in the kitchen, Mrs Snook having just this minute given him a small meal.'

He had taken his master's coat; now the professor said, 'Let Snook have that coat Charity,' and when she unbuttoned it Snook took it from her and said, 'This way,' and led her to a door beside the elegant staircase.

The kitchen was in the basement, a large room, cosy

and cheerful and equipped with pine cupboards and a
large old-fashioned dresser of the same wood. There
were rows of plates upon it, and copper saucepans
gleaming from shelves beside the Aga, in front of
which, in a comfortable basket, was the dog.

Charity stopped short. 'Two dogs,' she said
doubtfully.

Lying beside the basket containing the invalid was a
bull terrier, his chin resting on its rim, but he got up
as they went into the room and trotted over to the
professor who bent to pull an ear gently and scratch
the smooth head. 'Bertie,' he said. 'One of the family!
You like dogs?'

'Yes, I do.' She offered a fist and had it gently
examined before she went to look into the basket. The
dog lifted his head. He was still weary and his paws,
she saw with pity, were cut and sore, but he had lost
the hopeless air he had worn when she had first seen
him. She got down on her knees beside him and
stroked his grubby woollen head gently. 'What do you
suppose he is?' she asked.

The professor was sitting on his heels beside her
with Bertie pressed against him. 'Hard to say. Part
labrador, part sheep-dog I should think.' He looked up
at Snook. 'What would you say, Snook?'

'I dare say you are right, sir. He's big, and once
we've got him cleaned up properly and on his feet
we'll have a better chance of guessing. Bertie has taken
to him right enough.'

The professor nodded. He was examining the dog's
paws in large gentle hands. 'Poor brute—he's had a
rough time. Well, Charity, what shall we call him?'

She stroked the gaunt, mud-covered matted coat.
'He's so bony,' she said.

'Then we'll call him Bones.' He had his hand on

Bertie's head once more. 'We'll have to wait a day or two before we can clean him up . . .'

He stopped at the muffled peal of the door bell and Snook went away to answer it. He was back very quickly and there was someone behind him, pushing past him at the door, exclaiming impatiently, 'What on earth are you doing in the kitchen, Jake?'

The woman he was going to marry, thought Charity, looking over her shoulder and encountering a cold stare. 'And who is this?'

Professor Wyllie-Lyon got to his feet. 'Hallo, Brenda. This is my secretary, Charity Graham; Charity, Brenda Cornwallis.'

He didn't appear to notice Brenda's black looks. 'We rescued a dog from the street this morning—a nice beast once he's fit and well again.'

Miss Cornwallis went to peer down at the dog and then stood back with a look of distaste. 'It smells and it's filthy.'

'He,' said the professor softly. 'And if you had been wandering for days without food I'm sure you'd be filthy and smell, too.'

She looked outraged. 'Well, you'll have to get rid of him. There must be a dog's home . . .'

'Oh, no. He's to be one of the family—Bertie has taken to him and so have we.'

Just for a moment the lovely face was ugly with rage and then she shrugged. 'As long as I don't have to see it again.' She glanced at Charity. 'I'll wait in the drawing room—I expect this person is going soon?'

'When we've had a drink,' said the professor calmly, and turned a placid face towards Charity when she uttered a protest. 'And I'll drive you home, Charity.'

She waited until Brenda Cornwallis had gone,

banging the door behind her. 'No, thank you, Professor, I'd like to go home now.'

He gave an almost imperceptible nod to Snook and said smoothly. 'Of course, but do say goodbye to Bones first.'

She wanted to get away as quickly as possible but she had lost her heart to the grubby creature in the basket. She bent down and spoke to him and stroked his matted coat and then, since he seemed to expect it, did the same for Bertie.

The professor opened the kitchen door smartly, crossed the hall with her and helped her into her coat. As she was buttoning it up she saw him open a door and she glimpsed an open fire, soft lamplight shining on polished wood and Brenda's back.

'I'm taking Charity home,' he told the back placidly.

'I'll not wait.' Charity could hear the angry voice from where she stood. 'You can tell Snook to call a taxi for me.'

Charity didn't catch his low-voiced reply, but picked up her bag and went to the door to find the professor beside her in his overcoat and Snook opening it from outside.

'I really . . .' she began, but was bustled across the pavement and into the car before she could finish the sentence.

She said crossly as he got in beside her, 'This really will not do, Professor Wyllie-Lyon; I've disrupted your whole evening and upset Miss Cornwallis.'

His face was impassive and he ignored this completely. 'I have rather a splendid copy of John Donne to show your father,' he observed blandly. 'Perhaps I might have five minutes of his time.'

'Miss Cornwallis . . .' began Charity and subsided

under his silky, 'Mind your own business, Charity.'

It served the girl right, she thought, and surely she knew him well enough to know that she wouldn't get the better of him by being bossy. Charity closed her eyes; she knew exactly how to get round him if only she were given the chance. Wishful thinking.

The professor spent the evening closeted in her father's study, where the two of them were sustained by coffee and sandwiches and then beer and more sandwiches.

'The poor man must have missed his lunch,' observed Aunt Emily sympathetically. 'All that hard work, too, and then the poor little dog . . .'

Charity refilled their cups. 'He's a big dog and Professor Wyllie-Lyon has a lovely house with someone called Snook and his wife to run it for him. He would only need to say so, and I daresay a four-course meal would be put in front of him.'

'What is the house like?' asked her aunt. 'It's a splendid address.'

'Well, the hall is carpeted and there's a wall table and lights on the walls. The kitchen is large; it looks old-fashioned, but it isn't, if you know what I mean?'

'Never mind about the kitchen, dear; what about the sitting room, or was it the drawing room?'

'I don't know. I didn't go anywhere else but the hall and the kitchen.'

Aunt Emily paused, crochet hook poised. 'But, my dear, how very strange. Surely, the kitchen—I mean, I wouldn't ask the vicar there.' For such a mild, thoughtless little lady, she looked quite fierce. 'Doesn't he think you're good enough . . .'

Charity said calmly, 'Oh, no, it's not like that at all. We went to the kitchen to look at the dog and I'm sure we would have gone into the drawing room afterwards only this Miss Cornwallis was in there, having a tantrum.'

'Is he a ladies' man?' asked Aunt Emily all agog.

'No, Aunty, rumour has it that he intends to marry her.'

'How strange, I shouldn't have thought he was a man to countenance ill temper.'

'He's not. That's why he is spending the evening with Father.'

Aunt Emily's hook flashed in and out making incredibly difficult patterns. She said nothing but glanced at her niece curled up in the chair opposite her. Presently she observed, 'Sidney's engaged—the Johnsons' youngest daughter.'

'The one with the buck teeth? Doesn't she work in a bank?'

'Yes, dear. They're well suited.' She added delicately, 'You don't regret giving him up?'

'Not for one second.' Charity uncurled herself and stretched hugely. 'I'm off to bed, dear. The professor's going away for a day or two, so I'll be extra busy tomorrow.'

He didn't leave until almost midnight; she heard him drive away as she lay in bed. Far too late to see that detestable girl, she thought with deep satisfaction. And as far as she could remember from the day's agenda, all of tomorrow would be taken up with hospital rounds, a handful of patients and giving a last minute look to the papers he would be taking with him.

It was exactly as she thought; he was flying on an afternoon plane and there was no time for anything else but work. But perhaps he had gone to see Brenda last night, she thought uneasily, for he was so very cheerful despite the ordered haste during the morning.

A pity, she cogitated quietly, that it was impossible to tell from his calm face whether he was happy or not. She had never met anyone before who could disguise their feelings so successfully.

Certainly there was no vestige of ill humour on it when Mrs Kemp ushered in Dr Kemble.

'He wants to see the professor,' said Mrs Kemp. 'Can you slip him in?' And Charity had done just that, looking for signs of impatience or annoyance on his face and meeting with nothing but blandness. He said cheerfully, 'Ask him to come in, Charity—five minutes—I can't spare longer.'

She went back to her desk to be interrupted by Guy Kemble reappearing. He came and stood by the desk. 'My God, he's incredible! I've learnt more from him in a few weeks than in two years at home.'

A remark which made Charity almost burst with hidden pride. Her pleasure must have shown on her face for he said quickly, 'Take pity on a chap and have dinner with me, Charity? Christmas and all that.'

There wouldn't be much work while the professor was away. 'Yes, all right, I'd like that. It'll have to be while Professor Wyllie-Lyon is away though.'

'Great. The same place as last time? Tomorrow? Where shall we meet? Shall I come for you at your home?'

'No,' said Charity hastily; she could just see Aunt Emily's face . . . 'I'll meet you there, shall I?'

He went to the door. 'Tomorrow then, seven-thirty—I look forward to it.'

The professor's door was open and he was standing there listening. As Guy went away without seeing him, he wandered into her office, his hands in his pockets.

'Lady Burnett is waiting, sir,' said Charity, her voice a shade sharp; he had no business to be standing there looking as though he had never done a day's work in his life while there was a patient waiting. What was more regrettable was that he had been standing there listening.

'Ah, yes—Lady Burnett, a perfect example of hypochondria, Charity, and that is harder to cure than any number of other conditions. Half a dozen demanding children and just enough to live on would put things right.' And, before she could reply, 'What is young Kemble doing for Christmas?'

'I haven't the least idea,' said Charity frostily.

'He will be lonely, poor chap.' There was a silkiness in the professor's voice which she didn't much like.

'I imagine not. He must have made some friends here.'

That was a mistake. 'You, for instance?' asked the professor placidly.

'I hardly consider us to be friends. Professor, Lady Burnett . . .'

'Charity you are an echinus; harmless and pleasing to look at but very prickly.'

She gaped at him. 'What's an echinus?'

'A sea urchin.' He became all at once brisk and impersonal. 'Ask Lady Burnett to come in, will you?'

And the next time he came from his room it was to leave for the airport.

He was only to be away for two days, but they stretched before her like eternity. Even the pleasant evening out with Guy Kemble didn't help, although she did her best to be an amusing companion and a good listener to his plans. He had a great many of those and she bent a sympathetic ear to them, while he reiterated his future wife's charms and talents.

He took her home in a taxi and when she thanked

him for a delightful evening, rather solemnly shook her hand.

'I'll pop into Wigmore Street tomorrow if I may,' he suggested. 'I've still a couple of books to return; I'd like to do that before Christmas. I'm going to stay with Nathaniel'—the professor's registrar. 'Jolly decent of him and his wife to ask me.'

'I've only spoken to him once or twice but I thought he was nice. I'm sure you'll have a lovely time.'

They had parted at her door, much to Aunt Emily's disappointment. 'I had coffee all ready and stayed up,' she complained mildly. 'Why didn't you ask him in?'

Charity was mooning round the kitchen, wondering what the professor was doing, picturing him in some fashionable restaurant or at the theatre; perhaps Brenda was with him. 'I didn't think of it,' she said absently. 'Anyway, he is due for some lectures tomorrow morning; he wouldn't want to be kept up late.'

She glanced at her Aunt's downcast face and added bracingly, 'Look, love, he's going to be married the moment he gets back to New Zealand—he asks me out because he wants to talk to someone about her.'

Aunt Emily almost wrung her hands. 'Aren't there any unmarried men left?' she wanted to know.

'Oh, yes, but nowadays if they're not married they are having meaningful relationships, which as far as I can see are very much the same thing as long as they last.'

Aunt Emily, easily shockable, looked shocked now. Charity watched her prim, kind, elderly face and guessed what she was about to ask. She got up from her chair at the kitchen table and took her mug to the sink. 'Well, I must go to bed, I've plenty of work to do tomorrow and the professor will be back in the office

the day after that.' She kissed her aunt good night.
'And I'll have to be ready for him, with pencil poised;
he'll be rattling off memos and notes and letters full of
long words and expect them ready for him at the drop
of a hat.'

'You do like working for him?' Aunt Emily sounded
anxious.

'Oh, rather; besides, I get a marvellous salary, don't
I?'

She had reached the stairs when her aunt followed
her out of the kitchen. 'Charity, you're not staying
there just because of the money? I know I'm no good
at housekeeping and you are very generous. But if
you're not happy, never mind that; I'll manage
better . . .'

Charity turned round to kiss her aunt once more.
'Dear Aunt, I'm very happy. I like the work, it's
interesting. Besides, I'm to travel after Christmas,
aren't I? We must put our heads together about
clothes.'

The elderly face brightened and she went up to bed,
to lie awake and daydream foolishly until at length
common sense took over and she went to sleep.

The following day it snowed. Seasonal weather, said
everyone, and in the country it would be marvellous,
but here the streets were quickly covered in slush and
after a time the snow turned to icy sleet. Charity
nipped round to the coffee shop for her midday snack
and was glad to get back again. The rooms looked
cheerful and welcoming with the lights on and she had
almost nothing more to do. She would go home early
and spend the evening wrapping Christmas presents.
She made herself some tea and took it into the
professor's room and sat in his chair and stared at
Brenda's photo.

After a moment she said loudly, 'I don't like you—in fact I hate you, Brenda Cornwallis, and I don't believe you love Jake. If you did he'd look happy and he doesn't.' She was childish enough to pull a face at the lovely smiling one in the silver frame and then lay it face downwards on the desk while she thought about the professor. She missed his calm unhurried presence. What will it be like, she mused forlornly—if I feel like this now, when he's only gone away for a few days, how am I going to feel when I never see him again? For it will come to that . . .

She took her mug back to the cloakroom and tidied the little place and sat down at her desk to deal with the afternoon post, and that done, she sat back, allowing her thoughts to wander. Bones, the dog—the professor had mentioned him several times; he had settled down well and was fast returning to health and strength but there had been no suggestion that she should see the beast again. Indeed, after the unpleasantness at his house she very much doubted if the idea had even once entered his head. Anyway wild horses wouldn't drag her to his home again . . .

The telephone interrupted her thoughts then, and just as well. It was Patty reminding her that the wedding was on Saturday. 'I know you said you'd come but I just wanted to be sure. I expect Professor Wyllie-Lyon will give you a lift.'

'Well no,' said Charity carefully. 'It's a Saturday, Patty, we'll not be here. But I'll be at the church—I'm looking forward to it; I've even bought a new hat . . .'

'Super. See you then, and Mrs Kemp, of course.'

It still lacked twenty minutes before she could go home. It wasn't likely that anyone would phone so late in the afternoon but one couldn't be sure. She might as well make another cup of tea . . .

The kettle was boiling when she went to answer the doorbell. Guy Kemble stood outside and she beamed at him, glad of company even for a few minutes.

'Those papers I told you about; I've got them here, and the books.'

She held the door wide. 'Come in, I've just made myself some tea.'

They sat chatting comfortably; he had had letters from home and was eager to talk about them and she gave him her full attention so that neither of them heard the slight sound of a key in the lock and quiet footsteps on the carpeted floors. It was only when the professor opened his door and stood there, smiling at them, that they broke off their talk.

Charity got to her feet, not quite quick enough to suppress the delight in her face, although her, 'Good evening, sir,' was staid enough. But even as she uttered it she remembered with awful clarity that Brenda's photo was still on its face on his desk.

The professor watched the tell-tale expressions of her face with interest, although he said nothing. 'Guy, the very man I want to see,' he said easily. 'Can you spare me ten minutes? A most interesting case.' He paused and added, 'Unless I'm interrupting anything? Charity has finished for the day—perhaps you had something planned together?'

'Oh, Lord, no,' said Guy with an unflattering haste, so that the professor's fine mouth twitched. 'I'm entirely at your disposal. Charity and I had a night out together a couple of days ago; we'll have another one before Christmas.'

He was half-way to the professor's room and turned to wave a friendly careless hand at her; he didn't notice her frosty response, but the professor did. He wished her good night gravely. 'And if you could be here at eight o'clock?' he added. 'There's a mass of work.' Polite dismissal.

Her agreement to this was added in a wooden voice, as was her good night.

The rest of the evening reflected her waspish mood—she had to wait for a bus and then stand all the way and Aunt Emily had forgotten to put the shepherd's pie in the oven. Charity, much put out, munched bread and cheese while she laid the table and waited for the pie to cook and had great difficulty in keeping her temper when her aunt wanted to know if she was sickening for something. 'You look peaky, dear,' said her well-meaning relation. 'I dare say you work too hard; you need a nice little break.'

'Well, I shall have one on Saturday—it's Patty's wedding.' And that was an unfortunate remark, for her aunt wanted to know if she was going with the professor.

She was in the office by five to eight the following morning but the professor was already at his desk.

Even if she had wanted to, there was no time for anything but work; he kept her hard at it until after five o'clock and it was only as he finally gathered up his papers that he said, 'Can you be ready by half past ten on Saturday? I'll pick you up at your home.'

She said in a flurry, 'Oh, there's no need—I'll— That is, you will . . .'

'Is Guy giving you a lift?' His question was gently put.

'Guy? No. Is he invited? I didn't know he knew Patty. I can catch a bus . . .'

'My dear girl, you can't possibly go to a wedding by bus. Besides, being on your own isn't much fun.'

'No, but I thought Miss Cornwallis . . .'

He interrupted her firmly, 'Won't be going.' He

locked his door and stood waiting for her. 'Which reminds me, I'm taking her out to dinner tonight.'

'How nice,' said Charity inanely. 'To tell her all about your trip?'

'Lord, no, she has no interest in my work; hospitals and so forth make her feel ill.'

They went through the door together and she asked brightly, 'Was it successful and interesting?'

'Yes to both. Thank you for asking.'

He had shut the house door behind him and they were standing on the pavement. 'But . . . That is, I'm not being inquisitive, I'm interested.'

That made her sound like a prig and she blushed in the dark.

'A good thing, as you are my secretary,' he observed placidly, then added, 'Oh, by the way, Charity, when you see Mrs Weekes when she next comes to clean, ask her to put things back in their right places on my desk, will you? She left Brenda's photo on its face.'

Charity said at once, 'It wasn't Mrs Weekes, it was me.'

His glance flickered over her red face, and she went on quickly, 'If you'd rather not give me a lift tomorrow it won't matter.'

'Now why on earth do you say that?' he wanted to know. And when she didn't answer, he said easily, 'Mind you don't keep me waiting.'

She was ready and waiting for him long before she needed to be. She had put on a fine wool dress in a pleasing shade of green and topped it with a darker green coat, last year's but well cut and elegant, and to go with these she had perched a little velvet hat on her dark curls. It had cost a lot of money, more than she could afford, but it had been exactly right, just as her plain court shoes and gloves were right. Perhaps rather unimaginative, she thought, studiously looking at herself in the long mirror in her aunt's room, but there would be a great many people there and she wasn't an important guest.

The professor arrived at exactly half past ten, declined coffee offered by Aunt Emily, observed in his kindly way that Charity looked very nice, stuffed her into the car and began the drive back to Patty's part of the world. Charity, beyond saying hallo, had little to say; the sight of him in a morning coat had rather taken her breath. His elegance made her feel dowdy and she began to wish that she hadn't accepted Patty's invitation.

At the church she said a little breathlessly, 'Thank you very much; I'll look for Mrs Kemp . . .'

'You'll never find her.' He got out of the car and opened her door and held her fast with one hand, beaming down at her. 'Besides, weddings terrify me.'

She found herself in the church beside him, surrounded by mink coats and fantastic hats and whiffs of wildly expensive perfume. Just for a moment she felt out of her depth and she cast an unconsciously imploring look at the professor. His smile was kind and he took her hand in his and held it and bent to whisper, 'I'd rather be on the ward, or at my desk.' She smiled then, not believing him but grateful for his understanding.

Patty came swanning down the aisle presently, looking angelic, and everyone sang 'The voice that breathed o'er Eden' and then settled down with a rustle of silk and the swish of furs until finally the ceremony was over and Patty came back down the aisle, this time with her groom. She was smiling and nodding to friends and when they reached the pew where Charity was she winked at her.

It took some time to leave the church; Charity was surprised that Patty had so many friends and all a bit upper crust, too. She followed the professor meekly enough out to his car and got in beside him. She must really make it clear that she would make her own way home from the reception.

They were in a queue of cars, waiting hopefully to park, before she found the right words, only to meet with a mild, 'Do you object to me taking you home?'

'Of course not—I'm merely pointing out that it's a frightful waste of your time to drive back to St John's Wood when you live in the other direction.'

'There'll be champagne and those awful sandwiches which come apart the moment you start eating them. Perhaps your aunt would give us tea? We can leave once the happy pair have gone and I happen to know that they are catching a plane in a couple of hours.'

She had no chance to answer him; they had joined the line of well-wishers and Charity, not knowing anyone there other than Patty, murmured and mumbled and smiled while the Professor beside her seemed to know almost everyone there. And certainly he appeared to be enjoying himself.

Nevertheless, the bride and groom having been seen off, he edged her over to Patty's parents, pleaded work waiting for him, waited while she made her goodbyes, and popped her back into the car.

Aunt Emily offered tea the moment she opened the door to them. 'Hot buttered toast, scones and a nice fruit cake. So refreshing after champagne and caviare!' she remarked. 'How very nice you look, Professor Wyllie-Lyon. There's nothing like a top hat, I always say.'

Tea eaten, the professor showed no signs of going home; he accompanied his host to his study and didn't come out again until Charity went to tell them that supper was on the table.

It had been a lovely day, she thought sleepily, hours later. Jake was the most wonderful man she had ever or would ever meet; she loved him to distraction and just thinking of Brenda made her feel sick. It was a pity that she found it impossible to guess at his feelings, but he kept them so well hidden. He was always unfailingly kind and courteous towards her, although sometimes cool, and never once had he dropped his placid mask. She rolled herself into a ball, hugging her hot water bottle. It rather boiled down to the fact that he doted on his Brenda; after all, why should he display his private life to all and sundry? She was his secretary and she mustn't forget it. She had to do with his working life and that was the side of him she saw. The tiny glimpse she had had of him that day, so obviously knowing, and known by, almost everyone at the reception, only served to make the gulf between them wider. A tear or two trickled down her cheeks and she wiped them away impatiently. As far as she knew, no one had ever got the moon by crying for it.

She was to have a week's holiday at Christmas; the professor would go to the hospital as usual but he wasn't seeing private patients for those few days. Nothing more had been said about his trip to Norway; perhaps he had decided that he could manage without her, and somehow she couldn't summon the courage to ask. The few days before Christmas were busy ones and, beyond a casual remark about Bones, now turning into a splendid if vaguely bred dog, he had nothing to say to her. On Christmas Eve, the last patient ushered out, she and Mrs Kemp exchanged presents and produced small packages for the professor. 'I'll take mine in when I say good night,' said Mrs Kemp. 'I'm off now my dear, there is a mass of work at home . . .'

She disappeared into the professor's room and emerged presently looking pleased with herself, clutching a square parcel with an envelope tucked into it. She made the thumbs up as she went out of the door. 'See you in a week,' she said happily.

Charity covered her typewriter, tidied her desk and then fetched her coat. She supposed that she would have to do what Mrs Kemp had done; the possibility that the envelope contained a cheque disquieted her; to take money from him other than her salary was something she wasn't prepared to do. She stood dully fidgeting with the small box which contained his present—a leather-bound pocket book—and was relieved when his door opened and he came into the room.

He began without preamble. 'We go to Norway in three weeks' time. I'll give you the details later, but you'll need to get some warm clothing together in the meantime. You have a passport? Good. I'll take care of expenses, of course; you'll need spending money, though I must warn you that you will not have very much free time.' He smiled suddenly and her heart turned over. 'A happy Christmas, Charity.' He bent and kissed her cheek and put a thin flat package into her hands.

She thanked him with hard-won composure. 'And a happy Christmas to you, Professor.'

She wondered, as she said it, what he would be doing. His house packed with guests? Or perhaps he would be staying with Brenda? She had no idea and she would never know; his private life was so very private.

They went out together and said goodbye on the step. Christmas or no Christmas, a week without seeing him was going to be hard to bear. The minute she got home she opened his present: a Hermes scarf, a lovely thing of muted colours. She smoothed its silken folds and laid it away in a drawer with the unhappy thought that it was more than likely that Brenda had chosen it for him.

Christmas was quiet; church and turkey and Christmas pudding and opening presents. She had given Aunt Emily a little fur hat, something she had yearned for, and her father a gift token for an antiquarian shop he frequented. There were small presents from uncles and aunts and an odd cousin or two, people she hadn't seen for years but who always remembered Christmas. Her father had given her gloves and a cheque, and Aunt Emily had knitted her a sweater, a bulky one in dark blue which would come in very nicely for Norway.

The few friends who came in for drinks were elderly; they sat around drinking sherry and smiling at her kindly. They had all thought that she was going to marry Sidney and their sympathy for the supposed disappointment was palpable. She did her best to disillusion them but when she saw that it was hopeless received their attempts to condole with her as nicely as she knew how. And all the while she hugged to herself the delightful thought that in a very short time she would be going to Norway with Jake.

CHAPTER SIX

IT was a disappointment to Charity to find that when she returned to work after Christmas the professor had reverted to his calm aloofness. What was worse, he made no mention of the forthcoming trip to Norway, a mere fortnight away, in anticipation of which she had laid out more than she could afford on what she hoped was a suitable wardrobe for a cold climate. The cheque her father had given her for Christmas had swelled her purse sufficiently for her to buy a sheepskin jacket and now she was hard at work knitting a cap and scarf and gloves to go with it.

A fine thing if I'm not to go after all, she observed silently as she filed patients' notes. The professor, passing through her office on his way home and, as usual, leaving more work on her desk, wished her good night with aggravating placidity.

She wished him a rather snappy good morning when he arrived the following day and regretted it instantly when he said, 'Don't make any appointments after next week, Charity, and you'd better leave two weeks clear before booking anyone. We are flying to Oslo on the fourteenth—an evening plane, so be prepared to work that day. We'll go straight on from here.'

She would have to bring her case with her in the morning and be dressed for travel. Hardly what she would have chosen to do but she said meekly enough, 'Very well, sir,' and picked up her notebook and pencil and the small pile of notes, ready to start work.

He sat down at his desk and glanced through them. 'Excited?' he asked without looking up.

'Well, naturally I'm looking forward to seeing something of Norway.' She sounded prim and wished that she could be interesting and witty about it as Patty would have been.

'You'll see precious little but your typewriter for the first few days,' he pointed out. 'I hope you have got some warm clothes . . .'

'Yes, I have. Shall I need Norwegian money with me?'

He said carelessly, 'Oh, I'll see to all that. Just pack a bag and bring plenty of notebooks with you. They'll have a typewriter for you at whichever hospital we're at.'

She longed to ask exactly where they were going; not, she guessed, all the time in Oslo, but he opened the first patient's file and she took the hint.

She was kept hard at it for the next few days. The professor was seeing more patients than usual and there would be a formidable list to work off when he returned. And over and above that, Miss Hudson and her new assistant were still at odds so that Charity had a good deal of extra work to do. She didn't complain. Not that it would have been of any use if she had; the professor, a man of patient good humour, viewed the inconvenience to himself with tolerance and simply passed on the work that Miss Hudson didn't finish to Charity. He did it so nicely that she didn't mind and on two occasions when she had had to stay late, he had driven her home. She had offered him coffee on both occasions in a diffident voice and he had refused with what sounded like real regret. But that could have been wishful thinking.

She spent a good deal of her free time during the

week before they were to leave in selecting her clothes and packing them. One case, he had said, and she had no reason to believe that he hadn't meant just that. She would travel in a silk blouse and the new tweed skirt she had bought and wear a sweater under the sheepskin jacket. No hat, she decided, although the wool cap and scarf and gloves would be packed. A dark brown velvet skirt and a couple of satin blouses in jewel colours, slacks, another sweater and a second pleated skirt, plain court shoes, undies, dressing-gown and slippers were as much as she could fit in. More than enough, she decided; she didn't expect to have a social life and she had no idea what arrangements had been made for her. Perhaps other secretaries would be lodged together in some hotel handy for the hospital, wherever they were. It was a waste of time speculating; the professor hadn't made it very clear as to his own commitments. It didn't matter, she would see him each day.

Seen on her way by a vaguely loving parent and a fluttering aunt, she picked up her case, thankful that it was a clear day, even if cold, and went down the garden path on her way to the bus. Earlier than usual because of the case. But not so early that the professor wasn't waiting for her on the pavement outside, walking up and down with his hands in his pockets.

His good morning was placid and if he saw the surprise on her face he didn't comment upon it, but took her case and stowed it on the back seat and begged her to get in.

She hesitated as he opened the car door. 'I was going by bus,' she began inanely.

'I happened to be passing,' he told her smoothly and gave her an approving look. 'Sensibly dressed, I'm glad to see.'

She had been rather pleased with the sheepskin jacket and especially the long leather boots; probably in his eyes they were just what he had said they were, sensible; not at all the kind of thing the horrible Brenda would wear. If she ever went to Norway, thought Charity peevishly, she would take care to be swathed in fur from head to toe and wear boots made of the finest soft leather with spiky heels. But she wouldn't go anyway; she would wait in the professor's charming house and welcome him in something satin . . .

'I wonder what you are thinking?' observed the professor, glancing at her cross profile. 'Not regretting the trip, I hope?'

She hurried to reassure him. 'My goodness, no, I'm looking forward to it.'

'Good. Don't forget that we've a heavy day's work ahead of us before we leave.'

As though she needed reminding; twice as many patients as usual and he had a hospital round as well. She would miss lunch, she decided silently; Mrs Kemp could bring in a sandwich for her and she could make tea or coffee while he was at the hospital.

Beyond mentioning that Bones was turning into a normal, well-fed dog again, the professor had nothing more to say. Once at his consulting rooms he became immersed in his work, and she in hers.

She was tired by the time it was ready to tidy everything away. She rang her aunt, knowing that that lady would be on tenterhooks, made a cup of coffee and sat waiting for the professor to come back from the hospital. It was five o'clock and their flight left at half past six; she wasn't sure how long it would take to get to Heathrow but she had no doubt that the professor would get there in time. When he came without haste she offered him coffee, which he refused, and when he observed that it was time they left, put on her jacket and professed herself ready to go.

They made good time to the airport; outwardly calm but inwardly all agog, Charity watched him hand over the car to a waiting man, and then accompanied him silently as they went through the business of dealing with luggage, tickets and customs. Their flight had already been called; they went on board, settled themselves into the almost empty first-class compartment, fastened their seatbelts and sat back, Charity in some trepidation, waiting for take off.

It was ridiculous to have to admit it, but she hadn't flown before and since the professor hadn't asked her, she hadn't told him. Now she sat, her hands clasped tightly, starting in front of her, listening to the roar of the engines and not liking it very much.

'First time?' enquired the professor gently. 'Noisy, but only for a minute or two. Once we are airborne we shall be kept busy with dinner and drinks and one thing and another.'

He was reassuringly matter-of-fact about it and quite right. Presently they were served dinner and a glass of wine and coffee and once the trays had been cleared away he gave her a map of Oslo to study.

'We land at Fornebu, it's about six miles from Oslo. There'll be a car to take us to the hotel.' And at her enquiring look, 'The Holmenkollen Park Hotel; it's a little way out of the city. There's an electric train service but I'll have a car. Everyone speaks English so don't worry about making yourself understood.'

After that he buried his handsome nose in a sheaf of papers, leaving her to sit and think. Most of her thoughts were happy ones; ten days, perhaps two weeks, in his company, even though she would see nothing of him outside working hours. Just sitting beside him now was happiness, a quiet content at having him near. She allowed herself a little daydreaming and then took herself firmly to task and spent the rest of the flight studying the map of Oslo. She might love him to distraction but she was his secretary, someone to make out timetables and tell him where he was expected and how he could get there. She bent her head over the map, committing a good deal of it to heart, unaware that her companion, with a Norwegian mother, was not in the least in need of her painstaking help.

Cautioned to fasten seatbelts, she ventured to look out of the window. There were lights below, rushing up to meet her at a great rate, and she looked away again. But now she was prepared; take-off had been an experience, landing couldn't be all that different. It was, in fact, somewhat better, perhaps because the professor took one of her hands in his and held it reassuringly until they were on the ground.

There was a car waiting for them, a Volvo. Charity was ushered into it, thankful to get out of the cold night; thankful, too, for the sheepskin jacket.

It had been snowing, although the road was clear. The short drive to the hotel gave her little chance to look around her, but all the same the wooden villas and small houses standing among the birch trees on each side of the road delighted her. The city was below them, its lights twinkling, just as the stars above twinkled from the now clear sky. She was still gaping wordlessly when the professor turned the car into a short drive and stopped before the hotel.

It was a white building, lights streaming from its many windows, standing a little apart from the houses hugging the hillside around it. Charity got out and followed the professor inside, to be enveloped in a comfortable warmth and quiet luxury. They were expected, indeed the clerk behind the desk welcomed the professor as though he already knew him and, after giving her a civil good evening, addressed him in his own language. The professor, to her surpise, answered him in Norwegian and as they crossed the foyer to the lifts she asked diffidently, 'Do you speak Norwegian? Isn't it rather difficult?'

He smiled a little. 'My mother is Norwegian, so for me it is easy.'

She stood beside him in the lift, reflecting that she knew nothing about him at all.

Their rooms were on the first floor but at opposite ends of the wide corridor. The bell boy opened her door and put her case down, and the professor said, 'I'll be along in ten minutes. We'll have a sandwich and a drink before we turn in, shall we? We've an early start in the morning—breakfast at half-past seven and I'll want you to accompany me to the Riks-hospitalet. You'll need your notebook. You'll lunch there and come back here to do the typing—there will be a typewriter in your room. I'll show you the electric train terminal, it brings you within a short distance of the hotel. I'll have to stay on until the evening but I'll be back here for dinner.'

He nodded casually and went off with the bell boy, and she closed the door and went to sit down on the bed. The room was nice; large enough and most comfortably furnished, the window overlooking the lights of the city below, but just for the moment, suddenly apprehensive, she hardly noticed any of these things. Supposing she couldn't keep up with the shorthand or the typing? Supposing she couldn't find her way to this electric train he had mentioned?

Supposing she got into a situation where no one could understand her? She was still sitting there when there was a knock on the door and the professor came in.

'Ah, just as I thought,' he observed calmly, 'worrying your head into a tangle and making no attempt to do your face or to unpack.' He crossed the room and sat down in a comfortable chair by the window. 'Go and tidy yourself—the bathroom is that door in the corner—while I phone your aunt.'

He had picked up the phone on a sidetable and was already talking into it as she obediently did as he had told her. The bathroom was a splendid place, equipped with everything she could possibly need. She did her face and tidied her hair and went back into the room to find him still at his ease, talking to her father.

He held the phone out to her. 'Your aunt is waiting to speak to you.' He twinkled nicely at her. 'She wants to make sure that you are safe and sound.'

Aunt Emily twittered for several minutes until Charity's father took over, bade her good night and hung up. 'It was rather a long call—my aunt . . .' said Charity, 'she's—well, she's . . .'

'Aunts always are,' he pointed out placidly. 'Shall we have that sandwich?'

The food was delicious; open sandwiches and coffee, served in the grill room of the hotel. Charity, unexpectedly famished, ate every morsel, delicately drank two cups of coffee and, advised to go to bed by her companion, did so. She was asleep before her head had settled into the pillows.

Reviewing her day, twenty-four hours later, she was amazed at the amount of work she had crammed into a single day. She hadn't expected the lecture hall to be quite so full nor the professor's lecture to be so lengthy. Not only that, there had been a long session of questions and answers which had taxed her shorthand to its limits. Worse, after a short break for coffee, she had found herself taking more notes, this time while the professor conducted a teaching round.

She had lunched with three other girls, none of them English but all speaking it with enviable fluency, and then she had gone back for the afternoon session, to find the professor, having got his second wind, in splendid form.

She had spent a busy two hours until the session was over, and he, whom she had hardly seen all day, advised her briefly to get back to the hotel with the day's notes. One of the girls had shown her the way and she had gone straight to her room and started typing. She was still at it when the professor returned, knocked on her door and suggested that they might have dinner in half an hour and would she meet him in the bar downstairs. So she had left her typewriter, showered, and changed into the velvet skirt and one of the blouses, and gone to meet him.

He had offered her a drink and spent the whole of dinner discussing the day's happenings, asked her kindly if she had finished her typing and reminded her that it would be another busy day on the morrow. A remark which she took as a hint to get back to her typewriter.

She had finished at last and tumbled into bed and, now decidedly sleepy, thought that two weeks spent in a similar way would be just about as much as she could cope with. And hardly a chance to see Jake, let alone speak to him, she thought with regret as she closed her eyes.

But matters improved. After the first two or three days, some sort of pattern emerged; the afternoons, for an hour after lunch, were free and Charity found herself whisked away on a sight-seeing tour.

She had been urged into the car and driven to the ski jump, which she viewed with awe before enjoying the view of the city spread out below them, and the great spread of islands dotted in the fjord as far as the eye could see. It was a cold bright day, the snow crisp under their feet, and very still.

'Like it?' the professor wanted to know.

'Oh, it's super, and it doesn't seem foreign—I could live here . . .'

She turned to look at him, and surprised a look on his face which she couldn't read, only it disquieted her so that she added hastily, 'Of course, it's like home to you.'

'Indeed yes. Although my home, or rather, my mother's home, is some way away from here. Near a small town called Flam on the Sognefjord. We're driving up there next weekend.'

And at her doubtful look, 'You and I, Charity.'

She turned away to look at the incredible view. 'That's very kind of you to ask me, professor, but I'll be quite all right here. I can look at the shops and there are some lovely walks around Holmenkollen.'

He said impatiently, 'Time enough for you to do that; you need a break and so do I. Can you ski?'

'Me, ski? Heavens no, I haven't the faintest idea how to go on . . .'

'We'll teach you.' His glance raked her. 'You're a well-built girl and not timid, you'll soon pick it up.'

She wasn't sure that she liked being well-built. She said coldly, 'It hardly seems worthwhile.'

'Don't be a silly girl! You'll love it.' He turned away. 'Now, back to work.'

The following afternoon he took her to Vigeland

Park where she viewed the sculptured figures with awe, led rather briskly from one to the other by her companion, although she refused to be hurried when they reached the Monolith, a fifty-foot-high block of stone carved into over a hundred figures. And when she had done studying this, she wandered round the groups of figures about it, depicting life from the cradle to the grave. Standing by the final group, an old man and woman, holding each other close, she said soberly. 'That's how it should be; loving each other however old and wrinkled and weak,' and then quickly, in case he should consider her a prig, 'They are quite wonderful, thank you for bringing me.'

The professor wasn't free the following afternoon; he had a working lunch and, since she was well ahead with her work, she took a tram and went back to the Vigeland Park, where she wandered round in the snow at her leisure, staring wide-eyed at the statues, wishing that Jake was with her.

It was a cold day, the sky heavy with threatening snow, and presently she found her way to the tram again. There was some work waiting for her; she collected it and, since there was no message from the professor, took it back to the hotel and typed until their usual hour for dinner. There was still no sign of him, so she waited for a while and then went to the dining room where the waiter ushered her to a table, explaining that the professor had just phoned to say that he would be dining out.

She was a little shy of staying in the lounge after her meal, so she went back to her room and washed her hair and did her nails and wrote a long letter home.

They breakfasted together in the morning and since the professor made no mention of the evening, she held her tongue. It wasn't her business, she reminded herself; he must have family and friends since he was half Norwegian and he was free to do as he liked when he wasn't lecturing or in the conference hall. Looking back over the last few days she had to admit that he had had very little time to himself. And he had even less that day; so did she. She took shorthand notes until her hand was cramped and stiff, paused briefly for a sandwich and coffee and went doggedly on, spurred on by the splendid reception the professor's lengthy lectures were getting. She went back with him at the end of the afternoon, longing for tea and a bath, thankful that it was Saturday in the morning; at least she would be able to catch up with her typing. When he said casually, 'We are leaving for Flam early tomorrow morning. Shall we breakfast at eight o'clock and get away directly afterwards?' She let out a surprised breath.

'I can't possibly—I've piles of work . . .'

'There is nothing on until two o'clock on Monday afternoon. We'll drive back here in the morning and you can get it done then.'

She took a mental view of her pages of notes. 'No, I can't.' She did her best to keep disappointment out of her voice and only half succeeded.

'Then work for an hour or two after dinner.' He wasn't going to argue. She agreed; there would be several hours after the meal; if necessary she could type until the early hours.

They had a leisurely dinner in the almost full dining room, talking about the week and its happenings, and he encouraged her to talk about Oslo. Had she liked it? Was there anything she particularly wanted to see, or some place she wished to visit? 'And you will have some time to shop before we leave,' he assured her, 'although I expect you have noticed that things are very expensive.'

She had. 'Perhaps people earn more here?' she essayed.

'Yes, they do. But their silver and pewter are worth buying, and their famous sweaters.'

She had ventured to enquire the price of those on one of her brief visits to the shops. Once the price had been translated into pounds, she knew she couldn't afford one, but being handy with her knitting needles she had bought wool and a pattern, miraculously translated into English; when she was back home and had the time, she would knit a sweater for herself.

When they had had their coffee she excused herself on the grounds of being tired and bade him good night, a little peevish because he evinced no disappointment at being left to spend the rest of the evening on his own. Once they were back home, she mused, going to run a bath and getting her case from the wardrobe, she would make up her mind what to do; whether to go on working for him, seeing him each day, hiding her feelings, treasuring their rare moments of friendliness, or leaving and getting another job. The mere thought made her feel sick. She undressed, had her bath, packed her case with night things and the velvet skirt and a blouse and sat down in her dressing-gown and started to type her notes. She worked for a long time; that way she couldn't think about anything but her work, but if she went to bed she would only lie and think.

When, at last, she got into bed she didn't allow her thoughts to stray but kept them resolutely on the weekend ahead of her. She wasn't looking forward to it, although it would be super to see something of Norway, but the prospect of meeting the professor's family she found daunting. They would never have heard of her and she couldn't do any of the things the Norwegians did. She would be a fool on skis or skates, and she was pretty sure that if anyone suggested climbing a mountain she would disgrace herself. She eventually went to sleep and had a nightmare in which she was trying to catch up with Jake and Brenda, climbing with the speed of light ahead of her while she followed them in maddening slow motion.

In consequence she was a little pale in the morning and over the breakfast table the professor eyed her thoughtfully. 'You're tired—you certainly need a couple of days off. Well, fresh air and young company will put that right.'

He smiled kindly and bade her make a good breakfast and when she bent her head over her plate allowed himself a small smile.

It was still quite dark when they left but the sky was clear and the snow crisp under their feet. The professor threw their bags on to the back seat and drove carefully down the drive and on to the road.

'It's a matter of the best part of three hundred kilometres,' he told her. 'Main road almost all the way. We pick up the E 68 and go as far as Laerdal and then take a secondary road. It's beautiful country; I think— I hope you'll like it.'

Whatever the future held, the present was all she could wish for. They didn't talk much but as it grew lighter and the magnificent scenery became clearer, Charity got carried away with the splendour of it all. When they stopped for coffee after an hour she was bubbling over, gaping at the mountains around them, the stretches of clear dark water between them, and ahead of them more mountains, some with their snow-covered tops shrouded in cloud.

They had stopped at a small wooden hotel at the foot of a waterfall and she stood looking round her, taking great sniffs of the cold clear air. 'But why is there a hotel?' she asked. 'There is not a house within sight.'

'It's a favourite ski-run for weekenders and there are ski trails through the forest; the place is packed out on Saturday and Sunday during the winter and in the summer it's just full of campers and hikers.'

He took her arm and urged her indoors. 'Coffee, and not too long over it. I promised we'd be home for lunch.'

The coffee was delicious and so were the buns which came with it. Charity, anxious not to hold things up, made short work of them and then looked round the snug cosy room with its big wood-burning stove and wooden walls.

The professor said easily, 'It's through that door at the end, turn left.'

'I'll be quick,' she assured him. It struck her forcibly that Sidney would never have done that; what was more, she would have felt embarrassed if he had. She sighed. She had always imagined that being in love—head-over-heels and as unlike her tepid feelings for Sidney as chalk from cheese—was a mixture of roses and moonlight and soft music, but it wasn't; it was being comfortable with someone and not feeling complete unless they were with you. She sighed again; she would have to come to terms with the situation. As soon as they got back to England, she promised herself, and hurried back to where he was patiently waiting for her.

It was full daylight now, a clear bright day, the snow sparkling in the sun. Charity, pausing to take a quick look round before she got into the car, took a deep breath. 'It's heaven,' she said happily, and just for the moment it was, because the professor, holding the door open for her, bent his head to kiss her.

He shut the door on her, walked round the bonnet and got in beside her, and said placidly, 'Keep your eyes open, the scenery is quite something from now on.'

'Don't do that again,' said Charity severely, willing her heart to regain its steady beat.

He turned in his seat to look at her. 'Another word for Charity is love. Shall I call you that?'

Her heart became quite disorganised again. She said in a voice which shook because she couldn't breathe properly. 'Certainly not, Professor,' and then, because she loved him so much and everything was getting out of hand, 'Please—Please don't talk like that—do remember Brenda.'

He pressed the self-starter and sat listening to the engine. 'And where does Brenda come into it?' he asked gently.

'Well, of course she does, it's me who doesn't,' declared Charity ungrammatically. She made a great deal of effort to pull herself together. 'I expect you miss her?'

He was still looking at her, his mouth curved in a tender smile. 'When we get back home and there is time, we must have a little talk; I fancy that we have our wires crossed.'

He kissed her again, very gently. 'I do not like to be thwarted,' he observed with calm. And then drove on.

She was given no chance to think about that; he kept up a steady flow of conversation about their surroundings which meant that she had to listen to him.

She would have liked to have stopped in Laerdal, a large village, spread backwards from the fjord and into the narrow valley behind it. But the professor, after the briefest of pauses, drove on, taking a narrow road through towering mountains, their peaks snow covered, through tunnels cut into their heart until they reached Aurland, where the road ran beside the fjord once more.

Flam, as far as Charity could see, was mostly railway station, and a small one, at that. But it was very important, for it connected up with the railway to Oslo and had a busy ferry service to the villages along the Sojnefjord. The professor turned away from the ferry terminal and drove up a narrow road towards the village and then turned away from it to take a rough lane leading to the snow-covered slopes of the mountains. He was going slowly now over the packed snow, passing one or two houses set back from the track until he drove through open gates and stopped before a large wooden house standing on the lower slopes of the mountain, birch trees encircling it.

Charity got out of the door he had opened for her. There was an awful lot of snow; its vivid whiteness made the waters of the fjord seem dark. She studied the house and derived comfort from its solid appearance. It wasn't modern; it had a sloping roof and a square tower at one end, and an elaborate lattice-work porch, with a balcony covered in by glass above it.

He tucked an arm under hers and led her to the door, which opened as they reached it. Charity had tried to imagine Jake's mother, without success, but now that she saw her face to face, she saw that imagination would have been a waste of time. His mother was tall and slim, grey hair drawn back from a serene face, quiet eyes like his and the same slow smile.

Oh, dear, thought Charity, what a marvellous mother-in-law she would be; if only Brenda will appreciate her . . .

The professor flung a large arm round his mother's shoulders and kissed her and then, as an afterthought, kissed Charity; a light kiss on her cheek.

'And this is Miss Charity Graham, Mother.'

Mrs Wyllie-Lyon took Charity's hands in both of hers. 'My dear, I am so very pleased to meet you, and so, when they see you, will the rest of the family be. They're upstairs, cleaning up after some cross-country skiing. I've see to it that your skis are ready, Jake.'

'Good, and a pair for Charity?'

'Of course. You'll be an expert by the time you go, Charity; the entire family will see to that.'

Charity gave the professor a speaking look. She said coldly, 'I'm not sure that I could even stand up in them.'

'Oh, you'll have me to hold on to,' he told her easily. 'I'll put the car away, Mother, while you take Charity to her room. We're famished.'

They watched him walk away, both loving him.

Mrs Wyllie-Lyon led the way indoors. 'I don't live here all the time,' she explained as they crossed the wide hall with its wooden walls and floor, and started up the staircase. 'I've a home in England, too. Essex— a village called Tollesbury. Jake goes sailing on the Blackwater.'

They had reached a landing and Mrs Wyllie-Lyon put her hand on a door to open it and turned to look at Charity. 'You sail, my dear?'

Charity shook her head. She had no chance; she couldn't ski, she couldn't sail. She could type, of course, and a lot of use that was.

Her room was delightful, furnished simply but not,

she decided, cheaply, and with a view over the fjord which was breathtaking. She unpacked her case, inspected the bathroom, did her face and hair and went downstairs.

The professor was waiting for her, sitting on the bottom tread, with a very small girl on his knee. He got up and perched her on his shoulder and said, 'This is the youngest, Elsa; come and meet the rest.'

The large room seemed full of people, brothers and sisters and nieces and nephews, all apparently glad to see her. She drank the sherry she was offered and they trooped in to lunch, a buffet of cold dishes where everyone helped themselves. That eaten and coffee drunk, she was borne away to change into slacks and sweater, a woolly cap crammed on to her dark hair and someone's scarf wound round her neck and someone else's mitts pulled over her hands. She was to be taught to ski and the whole family wanted a share in the teaching. Jake was waiting for her again; they went outside into the winter sunshine and someone latched skis on to her boots and someone else thrust sticks into her hands.

The professor was beside her, vast in a bulky sweater, a woollen cap on his head and goggles over his eyes. He slid her own goggles over her eyes and said cheerfully, 'Now do exactly what I say . . .'

The skis had lives of their own. They crossed themselves endlessly and turned left when she wanted to go right, so she spent a great deal of time lying in the snow, to be hauled to her feet by obliging hands. All the same, after an hour she could at least stand upright and, even more, she could move very cautiously forward. What was more, she was enjoying herself. She was getting the hang of it very nicely when the professor declared that that was enough for the moment. The short day was closing in, anyway, as they went back into the house. 'Tomorrow we'll take the trail through the forest,' he told her. 'Very easy going.'

He unlatched her skis and set them against the wall of the house, and bent to take off his own. 'Well, yes, thank you,' said Charity, 'but don't you want to have a real run, or whatever you call it?'

He pushed his goggles up over his head and took a good look at her. 'Time enough for that, too,' he told her easily. 'Did you enjoy that?'

'Yes—Oh, yes, I did! I'd love to ski well—I mean swoop down through the forest and over the mountains, but of course I'll not get as far as that.'

Her companion grunted and turned away to look at the darkening sky. 'A good day tomorrow, I believe. We'll ski in the morning and after lunch I'll drive you over to Laerdal to see our famous Stave Church. Now—tea.'

It was a protracted meal, eaten in the living room with the grown-ups sitting at their ease in the comfortable chairs and the children on cushions and hassocks. And after tea, cleared away by a cheerful young girl, the ladies of the party fetched their embroidery and knitting and settled down to a cosy chat while the men went off to play billiards. Charity, thankful that she had had the foresight to bring her knitting, felt quite at home, especially when Jake's mother said in a pleased voice, 'I can see that you are good at handiwork, Charity. The winter may be long, but it doesn't seem so when we have busy fingers. You must try some of our embroidery.'

Charity had seen it in the shops in Oslo; fine stitchery, worked from a chart without a pattern. To please Jake's mother she was prepared to try anything.

She would buy a cushion cover or something and take it back home and when she was an old lady she would look at it and remember . . .

'You look sad,' declared one of Jake's sisters. 'Are you very sore from your ski lessons?'

Sore or not, she was prepared to try again after breakfast the following morning and this time it was easier, she wasn't scared any more, at least not on the gentle slope to which Jake had taken her. He pronounced himself very satisfied with her progress and presently left her in the willing hands of his older nephews and nieces and went swooping off with a younger brother. Charity watched them go rather sadly; she would never be able to skim along at such a speed and even if she could there wouldn't be much point in it for she wouldn't be here. She would have become lost in self-pity, only she forgot that she had her skis on and moved a foot, got entangled and fell over, to be hauled to her feet by little boys hooting with laughter. She laughed, too, and spent the next hour learning to go up a slope as well as down, quite forgetting to be unhappy.

After lunch Jake got the car out, declaring that she couldn't go back to England without seeing a Stave Church. And at her mystified look, 'Not far away. We'll drive back to Laerdal and go through the valley to Borgund; it's a main road and it will be open.'

She flew to get her jacket and pull her woolly cap over her ears.

It had clouded over and every now and then there was a flurry of snow.

'Tea about four o'clock,' warned Mrs Wyllie-Lyon as they went, 'and there is *eple kake*; I made it myself.'

Under the grey sky the snow-covered mountains

looked awesome. There was no wind and before they
got into the car they stood together in silence.

'A far cry from Wigmore Street,' said the professor
softly.

Charity nodded. 'A different world . . .'

'But you like it?'

'Oh, I love it.' She looked up into his calm face. 'No
buses, no queues; it must be heaven in the summer.'

He smiled a little. 'And heaven now,' she heard him
say softly, and then, 'Jump in.'

She was surprised to find that Laerdal was a good
deal larger than she had thought, its charming
wooden houses strung out along the valley at the end
of the fjord. At first there was the semblance of a
village, then the narrow streets petered out and there
was just one road, cleared of snow, running beside the
fast running river. The houses became more and more
scattered, although each one appeared prosperous and
self-sufficient, and even the most modest of them had
a double garage. Presently the mountains receded
behind snow-covered slopes and they passed a small
white-painted wooden church and Jake stopped the
car.

The Stave Church was close by, standing a little
way from the road, a strange pagoda-like building,
its many pointed roof adorned with fierce dragons'
heads.

'Why dragons?' asked Charity, and she tried not to
notice the professor's arm about her shoulders.

'Well, it was built in the twelfth century when the
people here weren't quite converted to Christianity, so
they played safe, built their churches and added the
dragons to ward off the devil of their heathen beliefs.
Come inside.'

It was almost dark there and very cold. 'They must

have frozen to death hearing mass,' observed the professor, 'and they had to stand, too.'

They went outside presently and crossed the road and walked briskly through the snow by the wild rushing river.

'Fish?' asked Charity.

'Salmon mostly—we own a stretch of water between here and Laerdal.'

They began to walk back to the car. 'Do you ever want to live here all the time?' Charity asked.

'When I am an old man and retired, perhaps, but only if my wife wanted to. But my work is in London and for the moment that's my life.'

Brenda would never consent to live in this lovely silent land, Charity thought, not if she were a hundred. And would she like his family? She longed to ask him if she had visited them, but she didn't dare.

They drove back through the tail end of daylight and the evening was spent talking. Getting ready for bed, she concluded that she knew more about Jake from his family than she had ever learned from him.

They made an early start in the morning but the family came downstairs all the same to say goodbye and when Charity thanked Mrs Wyllie-Lyon for her weekend that lady surprised her by saying, 'Oh, but we shall see you again on Saturday, Charity.'

And when she had cast an enquiring look at the professor he said placidly, 'I meant to mention it. We won't be leaving until Monday and you could do with another few skiing lessons.'

He swept her out to the car and drove away into the dark morning.

He was an easy person to talk to; she was quite at ease with him although at the back of her mind was the thought that very soon it would all have to end;

she would be his secretary again and he would retire behind his calm shell once more. There was no sign of that at the moment, though; he regaled her with tales of Trolls and Vikings and once they were back at the hotel he ushered her in, found a porter to take her bag, ordered coffee to be sent to her room and took himself off with the reminder that she should be at the hospital by two o'clock.

She took off her outdoor things, drank her coffee and uncovered her typewriter. If only they could have had a breakdown or a puncture, anything to have delayed them on the way; she enlarged on this pleasing idea for some minutes and then, catching sight of the time, sat down and began to type. After all, two o'clock wasn't more than a few hours away.

CHAPTER SEVEN

CHARITY, fortified by a sandwich lunch and more coffee, caught the electric train to the National Theatre, walked quickly through the streets to the hospital and presented herself at precisely two o'clock, ready for work, to find that her pleasant companion of the weekend had metamorphosed into a courteous, reserved and learned man, exactly like all the other learned men there. She hastily rearranged her pretty face into suitably serious lines and took care to address him as 'sir', not seeing the spark of laughter in his eyes.

She wasn't needed after four o'clock. She made her way back to the hotel, had tea and addressed herself once more to her typewriter. It was a couple of hours later when the desk phoned her to ask if the professor was available for a phone call.

'He is at the hospital still, as far as I know, but he could easily be over at the research centre or with one of the other members of the convention. Can I help?'

The voice was apologetic. 'A lady, telephoning from England, wishes to speak to him. Perhaps you might be able to help her?'

There were vague mutterings at the other end of the line and then a voice she hadn't expected, although she might have known.

'You are Professor Wyllie-Lyon's secretary? Well, I want to speak to him. Get hold of him for me and look sharp, will you?'

Charity quelled a desire to put the receiver back.

'I'm sorry, I don't know where he is. He should be back this evening—he usually leaves the hospital about six o'clock but quite often goes on to a meeting or a dinner. Perhaps you could telephone again later?'

'Who are you?' Brenda's voice held suspicion.

'The professor's secretary,' confirmed Charity and pulled a face at the receiver.

'Then do your job properly and ring the hospital.'

'Will you hang on while I go down to the desk and phone from there, Miss Cornwallis?'

'You know me?' The voice was sharp.

Charity bit back a variety of telling remarks. 'You will hold on?'

'Yes, but hurry up, I haven't all day.'

'Nor have I,' said Charity sweetly, 'and yes, we have met.'

She put down the receiver, ignoring the voice at the other end, and went down to the desk. It took a little time for the professor to be found and when at last he came to the phone he sounded coldly annoyed.

'Charity, what is so important that it can't wait until I get back this evening? Surely you can cope . . .'

'Of course I can cope,' said Charity snappishly. 'Miss Cornwallis insisted on you being found; she is waiting on the hotel phone . . .'

He broke in. 'Not here, in heaven's name?'

'Oh, of course not,' said Charity, snappier than ever, and then added, 'Sir. She asked me to find you, presumably it's urgent. Shall I give her your number?'

The professor said, 'Tell her I will ring her in an hour. Book me a call for seven o'clock, will you?' He wasn't annoyed any more, but his usual calm self.

Brenda wasted a few minutes telling her how inefficient she was and then hung up, but not before Charity, remembering to the last to be the perfect secretary, asked for her number. To be told, 'He knows it.'

She was covering her typewriter when the professor knocked and came in. It was five minutes to seven o'clock and she said at once, 'I have asked them to ring you in your room, Professor.'

He nodded and handed her a bundle of notes. 'If you could manage to get these typed before dinner?' he wanted to know.

She took the cover off her typewriter again, resigned to another hour's work, and felt the stirrings of temper when he added mildly, 'I've some letters—after dinner perhaps? I shan't want you in the morning, you could type them up then and let me have them at lunch.'

Her 'Certainly, sir', was uttered in a wooden voice which quite unknowingly made her feelings apparent.

The notes were almost unreadable; she was barely finished in time to have a quick shower and go down to dinner. As she reached the bottom of the staircase the professor appeared silently beside her. 'Time for a drink—you're late.' His tone was mild.

'Your notes weren't very clear,' she told him haughtily, not looking him in the eye because her heart would melt with love if she did.

They dined off *ansjos*—marinated sprats, *torsk*—cod, served with boiled potatoes and red cabbage, beautifully cooked with apples and spices, and *flotte vaffels*, served with cloudberries.

'A truly Norwegian meal,' commented the professor, urging her to try *geitost*—a brown cheese made from goat's milk and which she found unattractive. Nevertheless, because she loved him very much, she obediently ate it, helped down with Melba toast.

'And now, if you are ready?' suggested the professor. 'Just a few letters.'

Half a dozen, all of them full of long medical terms she would have to check for spelling. She wished him a sedate good night and watched him stroll away; doubtless to enjoy the rest of his evening.

'He pays me for it,' she muttered sharply and started in on the medical dictionary she never dared to be without.

Something she reminded herself about during the next day, for she was kept busy with barely time to take a quick walk near the hotel, what with the professor handing her scrawled notes and having to take down his lectures in shorthand, and having to spend a good deal of her evenings typing them.

But she had her reward on Wednesday. She hadn't been needed in the morning so that she had cleared her desk by midday, and there was nothing on the agenda for the afternoon; she would go shopping for presents, she decided, unless there was a message from the professor.

There was; the desk clerk handed her a note as she crossed the foyer to the dining room. A scrawl asking her to be in the foyer, ready to go out, at two o'clock. More work, she wondered and hurried over her lunch so that she had time to do her face and hair to their best advantage.

It was precisely on the hour as she reached the bottom of the stairs and the professor was waiting. His 'Good afternoon, Charity' was polite, but when he added, 'Shopping,' she gaped at him.

'Shopping? I thought—that is, I've got my notebook with me.'

'What a girl you are for work,' he observed blandly and took it from her and handed it to the desk clerk. 'I'm free this afternoon; a splendid opportunity to choose the gifts expected of me . . .'

'Miss Cornwallis,' said Charity quickly.

He said in a voice which sounded amused. 'She is already dealt with. We have Mrs Kemp, the office cleaner, the office porter, my housekeeper and Snook.' He urged her to the door and opened it on to the dusk of the grey afternoon. 'And you?' he asked as she got into the car. 'Do you not want to buy things?'

'Well, yes. As a matter of fact, as I'd finished early, I thought I would go to the shops.'

'Excellent—we can go together and you shall give me the benefit of your advice.'

He knew Oslo well for he drove to a car park and then walked her to the Hegdehaugsvn and Borgstadvn where there were a variety of shops of the better sort: boutiques squeezed between department stores, and all of them expensive.

A fact which didn't bother the professor. He purchased a small silver box, its lid enamelled with a wreath of coloured flowers, for Mrs Kemp, gloves, and a scarf for Mrs Weekes and cigars for the porter. He had asked Charity's advice about the box and she had fingered the delicate thing lovingly and in her turn bought an enamelled brooch for Aunt Emily and, since she couldn't resist it, canvas and embroidery silks for that lady to occupy herself with as a change from her crochet work.

'Mrs Kemp?' the professor wanted to know as they wandered along looking in the windows.

'A troll; I've seen some small ones, pewter, silvered over; and a painted wooden bowl for Mrs Weekes. There's the porter . . .'

'A giant box of matches for the cigars.' He took her arm. 'Let's have tea?' He crossed the street and opened the door of a *conditori* and sat her down at a table in the window. 'Tea and cakes? Now, what am I to get for the Snooks? Something special. Any ideas?'

'Do they live in your house? I mean, they have a home?'

'The basement is all theirs and they wouldn't move if you offered them Buckingham Palace. It's very cosy, too.'

'Then something for the home. I don't know how much you want to spend . . .'

'Don't worry about that. What would you choose, regardless of price?'

'Silver—a small dish—they can use it if they wish and it will never break or be smashed; and if they want to display it, it would look nice on a table or a sideboard.'

She poured their tea and waited for his answer. 'A nice idea, we'll go to David Andersen.' He passed her the plate of cakes. 'There is a busy day tomorrow— start at half past eight and on the go until the evening. You'll be hard at it until God knows when. I've a dinner engagement, too, and there is a farewell banquet the following night. A pity you can't come, too.'

She thought it prudent not to answer that. 'When do we leave on Monday?' she asked; regret at the very thought shot through her like an acute pain.

'We don't. We'll go to Flam on Saturday and spend Sunday there. We've both worked hard, we deserve a day off. We'll drive down to Bergen on Monday and spend the day there and fly back on Tuesday afternoon. Snook can meet us at Heathrow and we'll have an hour or two at the rooms before we go home.'

She agreed pleasantly, not that it would have made any difference at all if she had demurred. As it was, she was brimming over with delight, a feeling she kept sternly under control, although it was impossible to prevent the delighted shine in her eyes. Something the professor, an observant man, noticed.

They bought the silver dish and Charity lingered in the lovely shop, examining the magnificent jewellery and the splendid silverware; she could have spent an hour there, only it was closing time by now and besides, the professor murmured placidly that he was dining with several of the members of the seminar.

Back at the hotel there was nothing for her to do; the presents had been beautifully wrapped and tied in the various shops, all she needed to do was make a note of which was which, and stow them neatly in a drawer. She dined early, sitting alone at their usual table with a book for company, and then she went back to her room, washed her hair, and did her nails, and spent some time examining her face for the first sign of wrinkles and went early to bed. It had been a super afternoon. They got on so well together; she couldn't think of anyone else with whom she could be silent without feeling awkward about it. She sighed and fell asleep.

He had been quite right; the next day was a busy one. Half the time she didn't know where she was, whisked in the car from one building to another, making notes of names and meetings and a long discussion on sympathomimetic amines which left her with cramp in her hand and a complete ignorance of the subject. And by the time she had typed up her notes, the brief day had turned into early evening. She had dinner early again and went to bed with a book.

The last day, she reminded herself as she dressed in the morning. It was a lovely morning, still dark but with a clear starry sky and no wind. There had been snow during the night and it glistened in the lights from the hotel.

She found the professor already at breakfast and reading a letter, pages long. His good morning was polite but brief as he bent his head over his correspondence again. Charity helped herself to coffee, cracked an egg, buttered a slice of toast and unscrupulously peeped at a page he had flung down on to the table. A woman's writing—she was sure of that. Brenda, of course, and why this long letter after the phone call only a few days ago? And couldn't she have phoned him again? He tossed down a second sheet and she bent her gaze on the middle distance, to withdraw it smartly when he said quietly, 'Yes, it's from Brenda; you have no need to pretend that you are riveted by that appalling picture on the wall.'

He watched her cheeks gradually glow with colour and added, 'You look very pretty when you blush.'

She met his eyes squarely. 'I'm sorry, I had no business to pry. Is there anything special for today?' She was all at once the competent secretary. 'Shall you want me at the morning lectures?'

'No, I think not. They are by way of being farewell speeches. I think we've discussed everything worthwhile. But take a tape of the afternoon final session, will you, and type it up. There is the banquet this evening so you will have time to finish any outstanding work tonight. We will leave after breakfast.'

She transferred her gaze to her plate, anywhere but on the pages of the letter strewn around the table. The urge to snatch up a sheet and read it quite overwhelmed her. She hadn't realised that she was capable of such wicked ideas. Being in love was proving rather more complicated than she had imagined and certainly bringing out the worst in her. She finished her breakfast in silence and presently went back to her room to pack her things, mindful of the professor's injunction to present herself at the afternoon session and not be late. She never had been that; she threw him a reproachful glance as they parted but he didn't seem to see it.

Save for one or two brief businesslike exchanges, she didn't speak to him again that day; she made her own way back to the hotel at the end of the afternoon and settled down to her typing. There was more than enough to keep her busy. She did another hour's work then she decided to stop for dinner. She showered and changed and went down to the dining room and began her solitary meal. She was almost finished when she saw the professor, resplendent in tails and a white tie, crossing the foyer on his way out. He hadn't seen her. Indeed, she told herself with truth, he hadn't looked for her; there was no reason why he should. She went back upstairs presently, got into her dressing-gown and finished her work, did the remainder of her packing and went to bed.

She went down to breakfast at her usual time, to find him already there. His 'good morning' was affable with the brisk rider to the effect that they should leave as soon as possible as the weather wasn't too good. So she made short work of the meal, pronounced herself ready in ten minutes' time, and went off to get her things. A porter came to take her case while she was still taking a last survey of her person and she skipped hurriedly after him, anxious to start the day on a good footing. The professor had been silent at breakfast. A hangover? she wondered and thought it unlikely; more likely that he had had a phone call from Brenda—perhaps he was regretting his plan to spend another day in Norway before they returned home. In the car, once clear of the city, she voiced her idea and had it instantly and firmly squashed, and after a minute he surprised her very much by asking, 'Were you lonely last night, sitting there eating your dinner?'

She turned her gaze from the cold dark of the morning and stared at his calm profile. 'Me? Lonely? You didn't see me.'

'I saw you. The banquet was long-winded and highly indigestible and that includes both the food and the speeches.'

'Oh, did you make a speech?'

'Yes. I hope the weather doesn't break before we get in some skiing.' He glanced at her. 'The family are still there with Mother; you'll have plenty of help with your ski lessons.'

It sounded as though she would be handed over to the nephews and nieces; the horrid thought that perhaps Brenda would be there crossed her mind so that she could only mumble a reply.

They stopped for coffee as they had done the previous week and the wind cut like an icy knife as they got out of the car. It was lighter now but there were heavy clouds banked on the horizon and the professor observed, 'Snow, but we'll be home before it reaches us.'

All the same they didn't linger over coffee but drove on steadily until they reached the house. Charity, scanning the lowering sky, felt a pang of thankfulness that they had arrived; as they got out of the car a few flakes of snow drifted lazily down and they hurried indoors to a warm welcome.

Mrs Wyllie-Lyon kissed her warmly. 'You've had a busy week, I'm sure; now you shall enjoy yourself, my dear. This snow won't last—you will be able to go skiing after lunch.' She offered a cheek to her son. 'A successful week, Jake?'

'Yes, Mother.' Before he could say any more they were engulfed by the rest of the family, and, sure enough, by the time they had lunched the skies had cleared and the sun was shining.

Charity got into her slacks and woollies and went outside to where Jake was waiting with her skis. He latched them on for her, commanded some of the smaller fry to keep an eye on her while he went to get his own skis, and went round the corner of the house, leaving her poised on the crest of a long slope which ran almost to the fjord's edge.

Charity was never quite clear what happened next; she must have moved her feet, made some involuntary movement forward; she shot down the slope over the newly fallen snow, brandishing her sticks in a manner which might have given the casual observer the impression that she was an expert but to her was the only way in which she could summon help; terror had taken her tongue and it was her good fairy, not her skill, which kept her skis from tangling with each other.

The slope was a gentle one but it was still a slope, going downhill; it emerged on to what was during the summer months a road running alongside the fjord, but now the snow was deep enough to have covered everything to a depth of several feet; she saw, in one terrified glance, that there was nothing at all to stop her hurtling pell-mell into the smooth grey water ahead of her. She had very little breath but she used it now to cry for help; a silly squeak of sound, of no use at all. She closed her eyes, trying hard to remember what she must do with her feet to stop her headlong rush.

'You can't ski with your eyes shut,' said Jake loudly. 'Open them at once, turn your feet to the left and slow down.'

Sound advice which she should have heeded, but delight at finding him beside her was all she could think of; she turned a face alight with relief to him, crossed her skis and fell in an untidy heap, quite unable to get up. He pulled her to her feet and stood her upright.

'Not hurt? Good. But scared out of your wits, no doubt.' He put an arm around her and kissed her glowing cheek. 'Now we're going back up the slope again and this time you'll stop without falling over.'

Charity said with some heat, 'You're a monster—I'll do no such thing.'

'Scared? Don't be—I'll be beside you.'

There was really nothing to do but go back up the slope with him, placing her skis just so under his critical eye and then, her heart in her mouth, starting off down it once more.

But this time she discovered that she wasn't scared any more. Jake, enormous and sure of himself and her, was beside her and the worst that could happen would be that she might fall again. When he instructed her to stop she did. Rather untidily, but at least she kept her feet.

He was a hard taskmaster even if he was generous with his praises; they went back up the slope again and at the top he said, 'I'm going ahead of you—I shall be waiting for you at the bottom,' and not giving her time to protest he swept away with effortless ease. She glanced round her—there was quite an audience, smiling and encouraging her. When Jake gave her a shout, she took a deep breath and launched herself carefully. She had to remind herself several times that it was all right; he was there, waiting for her; she was quite safe. She gained speed and almost fell over at his 'Whoa there', but she managed to keep her feet, even if untidily.

'Very nice,' said the professor. 'We'll try the slope behind the house in the morning. Had enough?'

She surprised herself very much by saying that no, she hadn't. 'But I expect you want to go off on a long run. I'm fine now, I'll practice on that flat bit at the top.'

But he stayed with her until the brief daylight dimmed and they went indoors for tea, and after tea the entire family sat round the big circular table, playing Scrabble in Norwegian, everyone shamelessly cheating and helping Charity, declaring that it was a splendid way in which to learn the language.

There was a ski trail behind the house, winding in and out of the trees. A little too advanced for Charity, Jake allowed, though there was no reason why she shouldn't keep to the lower slopes of it, so she spent a couple of hours after breakfast working away with fine enthusiasm under his instruction, but when they went in for coffee she declared that she had had enough. Not true, actually, but it was their last day and surely Jake would want to have a few hours in which to ski without being lumbered by her clumsy efforts.

She watched them all disappearing into the trees behind the house and then went to sit with Mrs Wyllie-Lyon, who laid aside her knitting and proceeded to ask questions, put so disarmingly that Charity found herself answering them all without rancour.

'I shall be coming over to London in a few weeks' time,' observed Mrs Wyllie-Lyon, 'I dare say I shall see something of you, Charity.'

'Well, I don't suppose so,' said Charity doubtfully. 'I'm at Jake's rooms all day, but I'm working . . .'

'Jake lives close by, doesn't he?' enquired his mother artlessly, 'I expect you have seen his house.'

'Well, just to go in and see the dog he rescued . . .'

'Ah, yes, of course. You met the admirable Snook and his wife, I dare say.'

'Yes.'

'Jake has a great many friends. I sometimes feel that it is a great pity that he is so wrapped up in his work. He should marry and have a family.'

'But he is going to . . .' Charity stopped and went very red. 'I'm sorry; that's none of my business—Only something I heard—hospitals are hotbeds of gossip.'

Her hostess agreed gravely. 'Although I have never known Jake to take any notice of gossip. Do I sound revoltingly smug if I say that he is a good man?'

'He is, oh, he is—and I hope that he will be very happy when he marries.' Charity looked at her companion, her heart in her eyes, and that lady nodded her head and smiled slowly. 'He will be,' she said. 'He has always known what he wanted and when he gets it, he is content.'

Charity looked out of the window at the polished steel of the fjord, trying to imagine Brenda Cornwallis making Jake content for the rest of his life. Love, she was discovering, was an unpredictable emotion making no bones about disrupting anyone's life.

They left the following morning while it was still only half light, waved away by everyone in the house, and took the ferry to Gudvangen. It meant going down one arm of the fjord and up another but it was the only way to reach the road to Bergen and although it was bitterly cold the awesome scenery of towering mountains with here and there solitary houses hugging their foot more than compensated for cold hands and feet. At Gudvangen, Jake took her to the hotel on the small waterfront and plied her with hot coffee before they took to the road. He had said very little but somehow that didn't matter; it struck her that they had reached a stage in their friendship where talk didn't matter overmuch. They were at ease with each other and she wondered rather forlornly if that was the norm between employer and secretary, but the prospect of a day in Bergen with him was delightful enough to wipe out self-pity; she settled back beside him and prepared to enjoy the drive.

Bergen, when they reached it, delighted her. They had crossed by another ferry, coming into the town from the country behind it, and there had been only brief glimpses of the sea. Jake parked in front of the Hotel Norge close to a formal park and facing a square and he took her inside. They were expected. She was taken up to her room while he saw to their luggage and she barely had time to thrust her head out of the window to take a look round when the porter, followed by Jake, came in.

'A walk before lunch?' he asked as he tipped the man. 'The quay's only ten minutes away, we can stroll down and decide what we'll do this afternoon.' He gave her a brisk nod. 'Fifteen minutes downstairs in the foyer?'

When he had gone Charity explored her room. It was comfortable; more than that, luxurious, and the adjoining bathroom was the last word in elegance. She took off her coat and did her face and hair, crammed her woolly hat back on and went downstairs, eager to see all she could.

The wide main street, lined with shops, was pleasant and Jake pointed out the houses built on the side of the mountain behind the town. 'There's a funicular to Floien—that's the mountain you can just see. We'll go up there tomorrow. Now we are going to look at the market.' He walked her briskly past the shops down to the bottom of the street to the wide quay at the head of the fjord and then slowed his pace so that she might admire the flower stalls, carefully sheltered against the cold, and the fish stalls with their piles of prawns and neat rows of cod. The fjord was a hive of activity, with ferries crossing from one side of the harbour to the other, local ferries coming and going, and any number of fishing boats.

Charity, oblivious of the icy wind and the snow underfoot, stood and took it all in, listening to Jake's quiet voice telling her about the Bryggen—a row of medieval buildings facing the harbour—and King Haakon's Hall at the end of the wharf.

'What a bustling place—and in mid-winter too,' observed Charity.

'Well, the express coastal boats leave here each day—they sail to the very north as far as the Russian border. Five days there, five days back, but except in the tourist season most of the passengers only go from one port of call to the next, or perhaps to Trondheim—that takes two days.'

'I'd like that. Have you been?'

'Oh, yes—several times. It's the best way of reaching the villages in the north, although there is a good road all the way to North Cape, the ferries hold you up.'

She turned to take another look at the market. 'It's not like St John's Wood . . .'

The professor tucked an arm under hers and started walking her back to the hotel. 'Not in the least. You like it?'

'Oh, I do.' It was on the tip of her tongue to ask if Brenda liked it, too, but she stopped herself in time; only just, for he asked, 'You were about to say something?'

'No—Oh, no.'

'If you would like to we'll go to Troldhaugen, Edward Grieg's home—it's closed during the winter, but I know where the curator lives—I dare say he'll let us look round. We'll be back in time for you to shop if you want to. There'll be time to go up Floien in the morning before we drive to the airport.'

They lunched in the hotel restaurant: *gravlaks*—salt and sugar cured salmon flavoured with dill—served with a mustard sauce, and plain boiled potatoes which Charity had decided the Norwegians served with all their fish, followed by *riskrem*—boiled rice, whipped cream and raspberry sauce; so delicious that Charity had two helpings. It was not yet two o'clock by the time they had had their coffee. Troldhaugen was barely ten minutes' drive and proved to be a wooden house built in the typical Norwegian style and surrounded by a quite large garden, now buried under the snow. True to his word the professor went off to find the curator and the three of them wandered around the pleasantly cluttered rooms. 'It's as though Grieg had just got up from the piano and gone out for half an hour,' said Charity. The curator beamed at her. 'That is exactly what we hope those who come here will feel,' he told her.

From Troldhaugen they drove back to Bergen, this time leaving the main road and passing the Bergen residence of the royal family and then following the road until they joined the E68 once more. It was already dusk and cold; Jake parked the car at the hotel and crossed the square and ushered her into the warm and cheerfully lit tea room on its far side.

It resembled the kind of tea room it was so hard to find in England nowadays, with small tables, a counter loaded with cream cakes and bustling waitresses. What was more, the tea, when it arrived, came in a large pot, hot and strong. She beamed across the table at Jake, her cheeks glowing, her eyes sparkling, just for the moment gloriously happy.

She was happy for the rest of the day; they shopped in a light-hearted way before going back to the hotel, had a leisurely dinner and then danced. There wouldn't be another day like that one, thought Charity, lying in bed thinking about it. She would be home, in her own bed, twenty-four hours later and Jake would be Professor Wyllie-Lyon once more, and Brenda, so happily absent, would have become part of his life again. Charity, usually so sensible, had a good cry before she at length went to sleep.

She went down for breakfast heavy-eyed and with a faintly pink nose but the professor, after one quick glance, made no comment.

'We'll have to leave here about half past twelve. If you have your bag packed we can have a quick meal here before we go. Mrs Kemp will have tea for us when we get back.' He glanced outside. 'It's a splendid morning, though I think it might snow later. Wrap up warm, it's chilly on Floien.'

He chatted easily while they had breakfast and then bustled her away to get her outdoor things so that she had no time to think. They walked through the main street and turned off up a narrow side street leading to the funicular, a new way of travelling to Charity. She sat staring out of its window at the town unrolling itself below as the funicular climbed steadily up the side of the mountain. 'It's very high,' she said and was reassured by Jake's placid, 'And safe.' All the same, he took her hand in his and held it until they reached the top and then he tucked it under his arm and led her to the restaurant, sat her down at a table where the view was at its widest and loveliest and ordered coffee. They sat there for half an hour while he pointed out the various interesting buildings and presently they took one of the paths away from the restaurant, zig-zagging down to the town and walking back to the hotel through King Oscar's Gate. There they sat straight down to sandwiches and coffee before she went to tidy herself while her bag was fetched. Everything was going too fast, though, she thought unhappily, pulling her woolly cap down over her curly hair. In an hour or so they would be in the plane and these two weeks would be a lovely dream. She hurried down to the foyer and found the professor, un-concerned and calm. Anyone would think we were going to catch a number 10 bus, she thought peevishly, instead of a flight to Heathrow. He caught her eye and smiled faintly. 'There is plenty of time,' he told her soothingly.

The airport was some twelve miles to the south of Bergen and once they were clear of the town the country was beautiful. The drive ended all too soon; there they were in the small reception area, going through the customs, sped on their way to the plane. Charity wanted to turn round and go back. If only time would stand still . . .

The plane took off and she watched the snow-covered land beneath her merge into the sea. It was difficult not to burst into tears, and still more difficult when the professor undid his briefcase and, with a vague kindly smile, buried himself in a sheaf of papers.

CHAPTER EIGHT

It was as good a time as any to sort herself out; she must tuck away to the very back of her mind these last two weeks and remember that she was the professor's secretary. She might even, she decided, get out and about more often, meet some suitable man, and marry him, thus getting shot of the professor for ever. She was far too unhappy to realise the silliness of this so that the flight was largely taken up with the most improbable schemes. There was a short period of good sense when they were served tea and biscuits, but since the professor paused from his reading only long enough to consume these, make one or two commonplace remarks about the flight and then bury his nose in his papers again, she was left free once more to pursue her unhappy thoughts. She had come to no sensible solution by the time the plane began the descent to Heathrow.

Snook was waiting for them with the Bentley; he greeted them with Cockney warmth, stowed their bags in the boot and got in beside the professor after ushering Charity into the back seat, where she sat, a prey to unhappy thoughts, listening to him talking in a desultory, comfortable fashion with Snook. At the consulting rooms she got out and Snook slid into the driving seat.

'My case,' Charity pointed out. 'It's in the boot . . .'

'We'll pick it up later. A chance for you to see Bones. I'll drive you home.'

'There's no need . . .' began Charity, but she didn't

go on because the professor's face had assumed the bland expression which by now she knew covered a determination to have his own way.

Mrs Kemp was waiting for them, the kettle boiling and the teapot warmed.

'It's been lonely without you both, even though I've only been in and out as it were. There is a mass of post and I've written down the phone calls, Professor. Miss Cornwallis has phoned three times since I got here and that nice Dr Kemble twice—for you, Charity.'

Charity, taking off her jacket and cap turned to look at her. 'Me?' Somehow the phone calls made the professor seem even more remote; circumstances were hedging both of them in once more; the two weeks in Norway had been a lovely dream and that was all. She had better forget them smartly.

Mrs Kemp made the tea and Jake went to his consulting room and sat down at his desk and Mrs Kemp carried a cup into him, coming back with a handful of letters. 'You will have your hands full, love—here's the start of it. But have your tea first and tell me if you had a good time?'

'Super. A lovely hotel and a typewriter in my room . . .'

Mrs Kemp laughed. 'I bet you had your nose to the grindstone. I've made a lot of appointments. Will you have time to run through them before you go home?' She glanced at the clock.

'Yes, I'll make time.' Charity opened her bag and produced the troll. 'I thought you might like this— they're a bit like our Dartmoor pixies only they live in the mountains and only come out at night.'

They drank their tea quickly and Mrs Kemp said, 'I'll see if the professor wants me; if he doesn't I'll nip off home.'

She disappeared into his room and came out a few moments later. 'See you in the morning, love. Don't work too hard, now—tomorrow's another day.'

And a busy one, added Charity silently as she began on the post.

Jake's door was shut and it was very quiet; she worked steadily, sorting letters, bills, advertisements from pharmaceutical firms and reports from the Path. Lab, X-Ray department and outside doctors. She had them in neat piles when Jake opened the door, his coat over his arm.

'There's more on my desk,' he told her cheerfully. 'When you get here in the morning get them sorted out, will you? And be prepared to work late tomorrow. There is no one booked until eleven o'clock, is there? I'll go straight to the hospital—you'll find notes on the stuff in my room, so go ahead with as much as you can, will you?' She nodded and he smiled at her. 'Tired? Let's go?'

She hoped that Miss Cornwallis wasn't going to be at his house. There was no sign of her as they went in and Snook beamed at her and offered to take her coat.

'I've just come for my case, thank you, Snook, and to have a look at Bones and Bertie, of course.'

Snook looked disappointed as he opened the drawing-room door and ushered her in while the professor took off his coat, picked up the letters from the tray on the console table in the hall, and then followed her.

The room was beautiful, with a lofty ceiling adorned with delicate plaster work, a polished wood floor almost covered by an Aubusson tapestry-weave carpet in dim blues and greens and pinks, and a Regency striped paper. There was a handsome marble fireplace housing an eighteenth-century steel grate in which burned a cheerful fire, and the furniture was a pleasing partnership of comfortable armchairs, large sofas and a charming teapoy, a hanging cabinet against one wall and a chimney glass, after the style of Adam, above the fireplace. There was a Regency library table under the bow window at one end of the room and a pair of shield-back armchairs on either side of a handsome secretaire-bookcase, the whole lighted by wall sconces with delicate pink shades and several table lamps. Charity, studying her surroundings, heaved a sigh; a lovely room to come home to, and hard on that thought the more practical one that the electricity bill must be colossal.

The dogs were lying before the fire, side by side, but they got up at once when they saw the professor, rushing across the room to greet him. They turned their attention to Charity next, allowing her to rub their ears and stroke their heads. Bones no longer lived up to his name; he was positively chubby, his once rough coat sleek and silken. Charity knelt beside him while he made much of her and then turned her attention to Bertie in case he felt hurt. Apparently not; she scratched his head gently and he looked at her with the same bland good humour displayed by his master, standing idly, his hands in his pockets.

Charity got to her feet. 'He is positively handsome! they make a splendid couple,' she said, and in the same breath, 'I must go . . .'

The professor made no attempt to detain her but ushered her out again, the dogs with them this time. They sat side by side in the back of the car, as silent as Charity and the professor; only as they reached her door did he say, 'I dare say young Kemble has missed you, and you deserve some time off. Let me know if you want some free time and we'll see that we arrange some.'

'I don't want . . .' began Charity and stopped. Perhaps this was the solution to her problem; if Jake thought that she and Guy were serious, he might feel free to concentrate on his horrid Brenda. The small doubt she had tried to ignore for the last week or so, that he was sorry for her and had allowed their acquaintance to develop till it was a friendship as a consequence, became all of a sudden an overpowering one. She said sedately, 'That's very kind of you, Professor,' and, since it seemed rude not to do so, invited him in. He wouldn't accept anyway, he would rush off to Brenda . . .

He accepted with the air of a man who had been expecting to be asked anyway and followed her up the garden path, carrying the case, to be greeted by Aunt Emily in a fine state of excitement, and then by her father, who kissed her absently, expressing the hope that she had enjoyed herself and then turned to his guest with the news that he had acquired only that day a splendid example of an early number of *Punch* which he was sure would be of the greatest interest to him.

Charity, although a loving daughter, thought a number of unfilial thoughts as she watched Jake's broad back disappear into her father's study. Her aunt watched her thoughtfully, 'You must be hungry— there's a steak and kidney pudding ready to be eaten and an apple tart. Do you suppose he'll stay?'

Charity shook her head. 'No, dear, he'll want to spend the evening with Miss Cornwallis. He brought me home because we went straight to the consulting rooms and started on the post. There is a lot of catching up to do—I shall be late home for a few days.'

'You had a good time? We had your letters, of course, and your phone call, and the professor phoned at the end of the first week.'

'Did he? I didn't know.' Charity took off her outdoor things. 'I'll unpack presently. Shall I make coffee for us all?'

'It's ready. If you carry the tray into the sitting room I'll tell them.'

They came readily enough but Jake didn't stay long. He made gentle small talk with Aunt Emily, listened knowledgeably to her father's bibliophilism, reminded her that they had a busy day on the morrow, and took his leave. Charity went to the door with him, her polite thank you speech ready to trip off her tongue, but when she opened her mouth to say it he smiled down at her and said: 'No, don't embark on a thank you speech. It is I who should thank you.' He bent and kissed her surprised face, put his hand on the door handle and opened the door. 'Two weeks to remember,' he said, as he went out into the dark night and shut the door firmly behind him.

Eating her steak and kidney pudding, listening to her father and aunt's questions and answering them as best she might, unpacking her case and offering her presents, she pondered Jake's remark. The kiss she had decided to ignore; people kissed all the time, most of it meaningless—although it had meant a lot to her— but what exactly had he meant? By the time she was in bed she had decided that he had been referring to the success of the convention. After all, from what she could make out, he had made several speeches and given a number of successful lectures. Besides, he had seen his family, he would have plenty to remember. So had she, but she would wait to do that until the remembering didn't hurt quite so fiercely.

By the time Jake arrived at his rooms next day she had got herself nicely in hand. She had got up early, put on a sober wool dress with a white collar, brushed her curls smoothly into a french pleat, taken great care with her face and been at her desk half an hour early. She looked exactly as she had hoped she might, efficient, unflappable and pleasant in a quite impersonal way. So much so that when the professor came into her office he took one considered look at her and asked her if she were ill.

'Me? Ill? Of course not.' She had quite forgotten to be the perfect secretary for the moment; indeed she was in danger of slipping back into their easy friendship without a moment's thought and smiled at him enthusiastically, and enchantingly.

He studied her face in silence, a look on his own face which brought her to her senses sharply. She said quickly, in what she hoped was a very businesslike voice, 'I've sorted out the post, sir, it's on your desk. And a Mr Blake telephoned to make an appointment; he said that he had been a patient of yours six months ago and was anxious to consult you again.'

'Diverticular disease,' murmured the professor. 'You gave him an appointment?'

'Yes, he said it was urgent; I've squeezed him in before the first patient this afternoon.'

The professor nodded and disappeared into his consulting room, to ring for her presently and hand her a pile of letters. 'If you get on with these to start with?' He gave her his kind smile. 'I've scribbled notes for you. I'm going to Augustine's now, but I'll be back about one o'clock and will dictate the rest.'

She wouldn't be able to go out to lunch. Mrs Kemp went at midday and brought back sandwiches and Charity munched them as she typed. A good thing, too, for when the professor returned he wasted no time but began to dictate almost before she had her notebook open. When he had finished he looked at his watch. 'Mr Blake is coming at two-fifteen? I've half an hour. I'll be at the Berkeley if I'm needed urgently. Keep Mr Blake happy if I'm not back.'

He was gone, with the air of a man who had all the time in the world. Mrs Kemp, coming to check the examination room, went to look out of the window. 'There he goes,' she declared. 'I suppose that Brenda woman wants him to tag along for drinks or something. Can't think why he bothers . . .'

'Perhaps he loves her?'

Mrs Kemp gave a snort. 'No one could love that creature. Did you have enough to eat, love? I'm going to make a cup of tea—there is a busy afternoon coming up.'

Charity worked her way through the letters and then transferred her attention to the scrappy notes he had given her. By now she could read his awful writing quite easily; luckily, for her mind wasn't altogether on her work; it was busy imagining Jake tossing off gin and tonic in Brenda's company.

If that was what he had been doing, it hadn't improved his temper. Usually placid, he bore all the marks of an irritable man on his return. Charity took one look at him, fetched a cup of coffee and laid her finished work on his desk. But he spoke in his usual calm voice. 'Mr Blake is here?'

'Yes, sir.'

'Let's have him in.'

The afternoon wore on, the last patient went and minutes later the professor went, too. 'I'll be at Augustine's if you want me,' he told Charity from the door. 'I'll be back in an hour.'

Charity looked at the work still to do on her desk; she was going to be very late home, but he had already warned her of that and she in turn had warned Aunt Emily. The urge to fling everything out of the window was very strong; perhaps Jake felt like that about his patients. She accepted Mrs Kemp's offer of tea, wasted ten minutes describing the pleasures of her trip to that lady, finished the contents of the biscuit tin, bade Mrs Kemp good night as she left to catch her bus, and settled down to work again. She had almost finished when the professor came back, and as he came in the phone rang. It was Guy Kemble and Charity had said, 'Oh, hallo, Guy', before she could stop herself. He wanted to take her out; that evening perhaps? Tomorrow then? She said, 'impossible,' to both, trying not to notice the professor standing in his doorway, listening quite openly.

He came back to her desk while she was listening to Guy, who sounded excited and worried at the same time. 'Well . . .' she began and had the receiver taken gently from her.

'Guy? Wyllie-Lyon here. We're only just back and Charity has got a mass of work. Sorry about that but I'll see she is free by five o'clock on the day after tomorrow.' He handed back the receiver and went into his room and closed the door gently, leaving Charity fuming.

'Well, really!' she said tartly to Guy. 'Supposing I don't want to spend the evening with you? Whatever next? High-handed . . . interfering . . .'

'Hey, hold on. I think it's pretty decent of him. Do come, Charity, there is something I want to talk about.'

'Why me?'

'It's about you.'

'Oh, all right.' She knew she was being ungracious by reason of Jake's action. Possibly he thought he was doing her a favour; it wasn't likely that he knew about the girl waiting for Guy. She tossed her head, sending the curls flying. Let him think what he liked.

She rang off and the buzzer summoning her to the consulting room went. She picked up her notebook and pencil and went in, looking as cross as she felt, to be instantly disarmed by his, 'Sorry to keep you like this, Charity. Did you get some tea? We are catching up nicely with the paperwork; another day and we'll have done the worst.'

He dictated steadily, then finally leaned back in his chair. 'Right, can you manage that lot? I've some phoning to do. I'll drive you home.'

'Thank you, sir, but I can catch a bus.'

He smiled at her. 'Don't get on your high horse with me, Charity.' His voice was mild and faintly amused.

The letters were brief and took very little time. When she went in with them he was sitting with his feet on the desk, his eyes closed. He opened them as she laid the letters beside him. 'Did I ever tell you that you are a treasure, Charity?'

There were several answers to that but all she said in a prim voice was, 'I'm very happy working here, sir.'

'So am I. I hope it's for the same reason.' He began to sign the letters. 'Get your things on, I'll be ready in a couple of minutes.'

It was dark and chilly and she was tired. She sat beside him as he drove the Bentley to her home, saw her to her door, wished her good night and went away with the remark that he had a dinner date.

Well, of course he had, Charity told herself silently;

beautiful Brenda waiting for him, looking like a
fashion plate, no doubt, and probably making him
dance after dinner when all the dear man needed was a
good night's sleep. She ate her supper in the kitchen
because the others had had theirs and then she went to
bed. It would be another busy day tomorrow, she
explained to her aunt, but after that things would be
back to normal.

Things would never be normal again, she decided
sadly by the end of the next day. How could they be?
Taking dictation from the quiet man sitting at his
desk, intent upon his work, she couldn't help but
remember the feel of his arm around her as he had
guided her on her skis, the uproarious games of
Scrabble, and their day in Bergen. It seemed to her
that all these had been normal and now it wasn't
normal at all to be sitting there in the role of his
efficient secretary with no interest in him at all, saying
'Yes, sir, no, sir,' handing him his letters and his
patients' notes, answering the telephone. Worrying the
whole thing round and round in her unhappy head
when she ought to have been asleep, she almost made
up her mind to give in her notice. But if she did, how
could she live without seeing him? She couldn't.

She was reminded the next afternoon, quite
unnecessarily, that Guy Kemble would be taking her
out that evening and she was to leave on time. 'And no
reason why you shouldn't,' said the professor
cheerfully. 'I'm not coming back here after I've been
to Augustine's so go when you've finished.'

She thanked him politely and when he went
presently and paused to express the hope that she and
Guy would have a delightful evening together, and
that she had only to mention it if she wanted to leave
early at any future date, she thanked him again,

although this time the politeness was tinged with snappishness.

Aunt Emily was delighted that she was spending the evening with a young man and nothing Charity could say would persuade her that there wasn't romance in the air. Charity dressed without enthusiasm but she was careful to be ready by the time Guy came to fetch her. Aunt Emily hovering in the hall needed to be gently headed away from asking awkward questions.

Guy took her to Poon's in Lisle Street, a Chinese restaurant, and he was so bursting with pleasure about something or other, she hadn't the heart to tell him that she didn't much like Chinese food. So she ate her way through sweet and sour pork, rice and bamboo shoots and drank the wine she was offered and listened to what he had to tell her. He was really very young, she thought; she felt quite motherly towards him as he poured out his news. His Mary, dithering prudently on the brink of marriage, had written to say that she would marry him when he got back to New Zealand. 'I can't wait,' he assured her. 'I've only another week or two at Augustine's—I've enjoyed being here and the professor's been wonderfully decent and kind. There's that job waiting for me; we can get married just as soon as Mary says so.'

Charity beamed at him. 'That is marvellous news. Have you told anyone else? I mean, shouldn't the professor know?'

'I'm going to see him on Monday. I'll get a flight . . .' He embarked on a detailed list of all the things he had to do, which lasted through their coffee. He had so much to say that Charity was able to leave most of the talking to him and most of the food on her plate without him noticing. He was indeed in a blissful state of oblivion where she might have had two heads without him seeing them. She let him talk himself out, agreed for the tenth time or so that he was a lucky man and that he had a splendid future, and suggested diffidently that she should go home. 'It's been a long week,' she told him, 'and I'm rather tired.'

They were almost at the door of the restaurant when she saw Mrs Kemp sitting with two teenage boys and an older man. She waved and smiled, pointed her out to Guy, who waved, too, and then went to get her coat.

The return journey was taken up with a discussion as to a suitable gift to take Mary. Charity made helpful suggestions, thanked him for a delightful evening and wished him good night.

'You're no end of a nice girl,' he told her and gave her a brotherly clap on the shoulder. 'See you sometime on Monday.'

Aunt Emily was waiting up with coffee. 'You didn't bring him in,' she said accusingly.

'Well, he wouldn't have come, Aunty. He's in a hurry to get back to his digs so he can sit and dream about his girl in New Zealand.'

Aunt Emily was deflated. 'Oh, and I thought he might be Mr Right, dear.'

Charity poured coffee for them both. 'No, love. He is a nice lad but he doesn't give me even the smallest thrill.'

Her aunt looked disappointed. 'You are twenty-six,' she pointed out.

Just right for Jake, thought Charity; he was nearly ten years older than that. She smiled at the brief daydream floating round inside her head and Aunt Emily said quite sharply, 'I can't see much to smile about dear.'

Charity put down her cup and kissed her. No, love. Don't worry so much about me, I am all right.'

The professor had been back again after she had gone on Friday night and had left a handful of scrawled notes on her desk with, 'First thing on Monday, please,' written across the top one.

She was arranging them tidily ready for him to sign when Mrs Kemp arrived and, hard on her heels, the professor. They all wished each other good morning and Mrs Kemp went on in her breezy way, 'Did you have a nice time with that Dr Kemble? You had your heads together I must say. Plotting a wedding were you?'

'Yes,' said Charity and looked at Jake. There was nothing in his face to show if he minded, if he were interested even. He looked as calm and placid as usual and after a moment he went into his consulting room and closed the door.

There weren't many patients. When the first one arrived, she took the notes through with the patient's folder and laid them on his desk. He was sitting doing nothing, leaning back in his chair. He said, 'I am glad you enjoyed your evening.'

'I hate Chinese food,' she told him and watched him laugh.

'Well, that's a small, a very small consolation,' he observed. She glanced away from him and saw that Brenda's photo was no longer on his desk, and when she looked at him, 'Perhaps I have been a little premature, but no matter, I am a patient man, willing to let events take their course.'

Charity was quite out of her depth. She said inanely, 'Oh, yes—well, of course.' Then got herself out of the room, very cross because she hadn't the least idea what he was talking about and had made a witless reply worthy of a moron.

Guy Kemble arrived during the morning and, since the last of the patients had come and gone, was ushered straight into the consulting room. Within minutes the professor's voice over the intercom begged her to bring in coffee. Guy was talking but he broke off as she went in with the tray and the two men eyed her in a manner which made her feel strongly that they had been talking about her. She put down the tray silently, received the professor's thanks with a chilly nod and took herself back to her typewriter.

The two of them came out together presently and the professor paused long enough to tell her that they would be at Augustine's for the next hour or so. 'At what time is my first patient?' he wanted to know.

'Two o'clock, Lady Coreston. Then three others before a consultation at half past three—Mrs Brailey, Hampstead.'

He nodded his thanks and Guy said, 'I'd better say goodbye, Charity—I'm off very soon and I've a mass of stuff to see to.' He leant over the desk and kissed her. 'Nice knowing you—we'll look you up when we come to England.'

'Yes, do that. And all the best for the future.' She gave him a warm smile, then a brief one frosted round the edges in the direction of Jake, and poised her hands once more over the keys.

Mrs Kemp went out to lunch and the place seemed very quiet. Presently Charity got up and went into the consulting room and took another look at the desk. The photo had gone, there was no doubt about it.

She went for her own lunch when Mrs Kemp came back and when she got back Jake was in his room with the door open. As she sat down at her desk he called through, 'Charity? Bring in your notebook, will you?'

She took two letters and picked up a few notes to be typed, but before she could reach the door he said quietly, 'Sit down, Charity. There is no hurry for those.'

There was no help for it, she sat again.

'Did you know that Guy was going to marry this girl?'

'Yes. He told me the first time we went out to dinner. He wanted to tell someone about her, you see.'

'And you weren't—aren't in love with him?'

'Heavens above, no. And if I were,' she added coldly, 'it would be my business.'

'And mine. I don't know about you, Charity, but I begin to find this business of mixing work with pleasure a little tricky.'

'I'm not sure . . .' she began but he said slowly, 'I know. I did tell you that I was a patient man. We have to have that talk . . .'

The phone rang then and he answered it, put the receiver down and got to his feet. 'My registrar at Augustine's wants me over there at once. Say all the right things to Lady Coreston if I'm not back.' He had gone while she was framing a 'yes, sir'.

He wasn't back. Exerting all her charm to keep Lady Coreston in a good frame of mind, Charity kept a longing eye on the clock and listened with half an ear to that lady recounting her symptoms yet again. They were quite nasty ones and it seemed likely that the professor would come up with an equally nasty diagnosis, even if it was wrapped up kindly and delivered with a genuine sympathy. When he did come, whatever serious happening had kept him so long at the hospital had been successfully concealed behind his placid manner. Charity handed the patient over to him and went back to her typing. Mrs Kemp interrupted her to tell her in a hissing whisper that they were running half an hour late and had she forgotten that the professor was to go to Mrs Brailey at half past three.

Charity looked at the clock again. 'If he takes five minutes off each consultation and gets there fifteen minutes late, he could manage it.'

A little muddled, perhaps, but Mrs Kemp understood at once. 'When Lady Coreston comes out, I'll hang on to the next one till you've had time to pop in and suggest it.'

She slid away, her old-fashioned starched apron crackling, and presently Charity did as she suggested, tapping on his door and whisking in, to pause at the sight of him sitting back in his chair with his eyes shut.

'Are you ill? Shall I get you something? Tea, coffee? You work too hard.'

The words tumbled out and she would have given worlds to have got them back again as he opened his eyes and smiled at her, his eyebrows lifted in faint mockery. 'Such concern,' he observed softly.

She ignored that and repeated her plan in a rough and ready fashion. 'If I phoned through to Mrs Brailey's house,' she offered, 'and said you'd be fifteen minutes late, unavoidably detained and all that . . .'

'I do not know how I got through my days before I encountered you, Charity. By all means go ahead with your scheme, though I'm not promising to keep to your timetable.'

She had to be content with that, and at least she was able to let Mrs Brailey know. The afternoon wore on and she got him away a good deal later than the fifteen minutes she had bargained for. Still, he had gone, seemingly unhurried, laying a little pile of notes on her desk as he passed. She would be late home yet again.

She had finished all she had to do and was making tea for Mrs Kemp and herself when the professor rang to say that he was back at Augustine's and wouldn't be in again that evening. She was to go home as soon as she had finished and locked up.

Mrs Kemp, already hatted and coated, drank her tea, gave her opinion that the professor was burning the candle at both ends and nothing good would come of it, and started to hunt in her handbag for change for the bus.

'What do you mean? The candle at both ends?'

'Well, love, that girl he's supposed to be marrying—though I don't see it happening, mind you—she's a real night bird, always wanting to go dancing and wining and dining. My Mrs Chubb who obliges twice a week, she's a friend of Mrs Snook and she lets a word or two drop now and then. They've had a bit of a tiff, she thinks, or that Miss Cornwallis is away.' She sniffed. 'I wouldn't give her house room. After his money, I don't doubt.'

She turned her motherly gaze on Charity. 'And that nice Dr Kemble? Has he gone back to New Zealand? I quite thought it was a case with him, love; I'm disappointed.'

'He told me the first time that we met that he had a girl at home. Besides, Mrs Kemp, he is so young I never gave him a thought . . .'

'Lost your heart already, haven't you?' Mrs Kemp got to her feet. 'OK, I'm not prying. See you in the morning.' She beamed in her friendly way. 'Bye for now.'

Presently Charity tidied her desk, locked up, put on her outdoor things and left too. Outside the front door she discovered that the faint drizzle had turned to an icy rain. It had got much colder, too; under her feet the pavement felt slippery with a thin coating of ice. She made her way to the bus stop, skidding a bit as she went and then stood at the tail end of a long queue, getting very wet as two buses, already full up, went past. She whiled away the time with improbable ideas. The most important one was that Jake should come past the queue and see her, give her a lift and on the way home tell her that he had given up Brenda and had fallen in love with her instead. She hadn't decided what she would say when she was brought back to real life by a sharp elbow in her ribs.

'Get a move on, then,' said an aggrieved voice behind her. 'If you want ter get on the bus, then fer 'eaven's sake get a move on.'

The bus was full. Charity, sandwiched between two stout ladies with plastic Harrod's shopping bags and important hats, listened to the conversation which they carried on across her. They had had a nice day, she gathered, finding just the right thing for the cruise and how fortunate that they were both going to Amanda's dinner party. Amanda, a mutual friend, had got fat; the two ladies had a lovely time discussing her shortcomings and Charity had a lovely time listening to them, until she caught the eye of one of them.

'Such a pity we couldn't find a taxi,' said the owner of the eye, 'buses are so public. I mean . . .' She gave Charity a smouldering look.

'Of course they are,' said Charity matter-of-factly. 'They are public transport.'

The bus stopped to let a handful of people off and two handfuls get on, youths with startling hairstyles and black leather jackets. They had loud voices and the two ladies stopped talking to listen to them.

Probably they meant no harm; they began to jostle each other and then those around them, and when the conductor told them to get off they refused. Reinforced by the driver, he tried again with the bus standing at the side of the road while passengers, only too anxious to get off, were hindered by the boys on the step. No one was prepared for the sudden jolt as the bus started off, leaving the conductor and driver standing on the kerb. The boys were still on the platform, roaring their heads off at the joke.

'That's Charlie—fancies 'iself drivin' 'e does,' one of the youths shouted, 'Ave yer all 'ome in no time.'

It had all happened so quickly and, as luck would have it, there had been no one much to see what had happened. Charity, supported physically at least by the ladies on either side of her, swallowed down a nasty feeling of panic and told herself that it couldn't last long.

It didn't; the driver decided to cut across the traffic and go through the traffic lights at the same time as a heavily loaded lorry was, quite legitimately, obeying the green light. Going slowly and driven by a level-headed man, it swerved to avoid the bus, gave it an unavoidable glancing blow and pulled up at the side of the street past the lights. Not so the bus; the boy had lost his head and slammed on the brakes. They came to a sudden lurching stop so that the passengers went in all directions. Charity, welded as it were to her two companions, fell with them into a heap on the floor. They were both screaming in a refined sort of way and one of the important hats had left its owner's head and was clutched fast in Charity's hand. For a moment she lay sprawling, but the general surge of the other passengers struggling to their feet got her upright, too. Her fear had given way to ill temper at finding herself in such a situation. She hauled the two ladies to their feet with some difficulty, told them crossly to stop making such a noise, jammed the hat back on its owner's head and looked around her. There was a great deal of pushing and shoving and people calling each other, and up by the door she saw with relief a policeman's helmeted head. Several voices were shouting, 'Don't panic!' and there was a slow erratic movement towards the door. Everything was going very nicely as far as she could see from her cramped position. There was glass tinkling, police sirens wailing and a faint smell of burning. She sniffed the air and almost bit her tongue off, so as not to shout 'Fire!' Probably it was the brakes, and a good half of the passengers were off the bus by now; to panic wouldn't help. Besides, she had a sensitive nose; she could be fancying it.

There was a stout man in front of her and a motley collection of housewives, girls going home from the office and one or two idle city gents hedging her in. The stout man suddenly bellowed 'Fire!' and there was an instant forward movement from those at the back, naturally enough anxious to get off as quickly as possible. But the bus platform was small and there were quite a few elderly people who couldn't hurry, fire or no fire. The pressure behind Charity increased and the stout man, turning suddenly, drove an elbow into her eye. It threw her off balance and she was pushed aside. For the moment she didn't mind; all she wanted to do was to be sick and lie somewhere until the pain was better. There was nowhere to lie; she was carried slowly forward with the rearguard of the passengers and two of the city gents caught her by the arms and trundled her as fast as possible to the door. They were the last to leave the bus. There were a lot of people by now, an ambulance or two, and several police cars.

'She'll need a bit of attention,' she heard someone say and found herself wedged into an ambulance with several other people, all rather the worse for wear. 'I am quite able to go home,' she protested to a policeman urging her in.

He studied her rapidly swelling eye. 'A bit of treatment won't come amiss,' he told her kindly, 'and then you'll be able to go home.'

The ambulance took them to Augustine's. Charity, the last to get in, was the first to get out. The professor, crossing the courtyard to his car, had a splendid view of her, standing obediently where the ambulance had deposited her. His firm mouth twitched into a faint, tender smile but there was concern in his eyes. He reached her just before the ambulance man reached her. 'My poor darling, whatever has happened?' And then, 'It's all right, she's been on the staff here—I'll take her over.'

His arm felt comforting as he led her into the Accident Centre. He lifted a finger and a staff nurse came hurrying over to him. 'My secretary—seems to have got involved in an accident. I'll take a look at her—that's a nasty eye. Can you be spared, Staff?'

'Yes, sir. It's a bus crash, some boys drove off with it and crashed it. No one is badly hurt.'

'Good. Let's get Charity's coat off and make her comfortable on the couch while I have a word with Sister.'

Sister came back with him and sent Staff back to join the junior sister and the other nurse. She knew Charity by sight and tut-tutted in a motherly way when she saw the eye, wondering why Professor Wyllic-Lyon, usually so placid and unflappable, was so concerned. She scented romance although there was nothing in his manner to indicate that. His soft-voiced directions were delivered in his usual calm way but there was no doubt that Charity's one good eye was fastened upon his face with a quite painful intensity.

She was examined gently and her rapidly closing eye treated, and then she was helped off the couch again. She felt grubby and untidy and shaky but she thanked them both and started out of the cubicle. 'A taxi?' suggested Sister.

'I'll take Charity home,' said the professor, adding, 'Many thanks, Sister.'

There were still people in the Accident Centre having cuts and bruises treated. There were several policemen there, too. The professor gave one of them her name and address and took her out to the car.

'I'm perfectly able . . .' began Charity.

She was ignored, stuffed gently into the front seat and told to close her remaining good eye, something she was glad to do. She opened it when the car stopped and sat up with a jerk. 'This is your house,' she pointed out.

'Yes.' An unsatisfactory answer, but her head ached and she couldn't be bothered to pursue the matter. He put an arm round her and led her indoors to be met by Snook, who took one look and went to fetch Mrs Snook.

The professor sat her down in a chair and she leaned back with her eye closed again, not caring what was to happen next. She heard his voice clearly enough though.

'You will stay here, Charity. Mrs Snook will help you to bed. I am about to ring your aunt and ask her to come here to be with you until you are fit to go home.'

'I'm all right,' she mumbled.

'My dear girl, have you seen that eye?' He sounded amused.

And after that she didn't remember much; being undressed by a kindly Mrs Snook, shrouded in a roomy nightgown and eased gently into a warm bed and bidden to drink her hot milk like a good girl. Headache or not, she was asleep in no time at all. The professor, coming in to take a look at her, studied her swollen reddened eye and then bent and kissed her gently. Then he went downstairs to await Aunt Emily, whom Snook had gone to fetch with the car. He had had a word with Charity's father, too, assuring him gravely that Charity would be perfectly safe with him.

'Well, of course she will,' said Mr Graham testily. 'I'm not a half blind fool.'

CHAPTER NINE

CHARITY slept all night and woke to find Aunt Emily and the professor standing at the foot of the bed, looking at her. The damaged eye was still swollen and shut but the good one was bright enough.

'Better?' asked the professor and, when she nodded, 'Good. You will stay in bed today, Charity. When you have had a cup of tea, I will come and take a look at that eye.' He smiled and then went away and her aunt said, 'Such a kind, good man. I have the room next to this one, love, and every possible thing I could need. I must say it was a shock when he told us, but you are in the best possible hands. Here is your tea,' she added unnecessarily and Charity obediently drank it, watched by her aunt and Mrs Snook.

'What's the time?' she asked, and then, 'He'll be late—there is a patient coming at nine o'clock . . .'

The two ladies made soothing noises and disappeared and the professor was there instead. He came and sat on the edge of the bed and examined her eye with care. 'Painful?' he wanted to know. 'Headache still?' He produced an ophthalmoscope. 'This is going to be uncomfortable. I want to make sure that there is no damage to your eye.'

When he had finished he said, 'Good girl. Everything is as it should be. We'll deal with the swelling and you will be fine in a few days. You will have to wear a patch for a day or two once the swelling has gone down.'

He got up and went to the door. 'Sleep all you can, you had a nasty shock.'

He had gone, leaving her to lie there quite deflated by his impersonal manner. But it was impossible to stay that way; her aunt and Mrs Snook, bearing a splendid breakfast between them, came back again and stayed there making sure that she ate a sizeable portion of it.

Only then was she permitted to take a bath and put on one of her own nightgowns to come back to a freshly made bed and her aunt waiting with two pills and a glass of water.

'Jake says you are to take these, dear.'

'I don't need them,' Charity slid under the soft light blankets.

'That's not for you or me to say,' said Aunt Emily with unexpected firmness. 'If Jake says you are to take them, then you'll do so, Charity.' And, when Charity had reluctantly swallowed them, 'Now you will have another nice nap and Mrs Snook will bring you a nice hot drink presently. Such a good woman—Jake has two treasures in her and Snook. And this is a beautiful house.' Aunt Emily bent and kissed her niece, something she seldom did. 'Dear child—how thankful your father and I are that Jake saw you . . .'

Charity went to sleep again to wake and find Mrs Snook's kindly face looking down on her. 'I came up with your coffee, but you were so sound asleep. Now there is a nice bit of lunch for you. Just let me shake up those pillows.'

So Charity sat up obediently and, when her lunch came, ate it up, protesting that she was perfectly able to get up and go home.

'Yes, dear, and I'm glad you feel more the thing, but we must wait and see what Jake says.' Aunt Emily

removed the tray, smoothed the sheets and advised her
to have another nice rest. 'And I'll bring you a cup of
tea in an hour or two.'

Charity watched the door close behind her aunt and
looked at her watch. It was barely two o'clock; the
household, she guessed, would take a rest for an hour
or so. She got out of bed, frowning a little at the pain
around her eye. But that didn't stop her from
exploring the room.

It was a charming place with its magnificent
mahogany bed and a sofa table of the same wood in the
bay window. There was a triple mirror on it and
Charity went to have a look. It was worse than she had
thought; they had given her a patch to put over her
eye but the skin around it was a rich purple. No make-
up, of course, and her hair in a tangle of curls. A real
fright. She pulled a hideous face at her reflection and
went on with her exploring. There was a tallboy
against one wall and a door beside it. It led to the
bathroom she had used earlier that day and had hardly
noticed; now she examined it at her leisure: its pearly-
pink tiled walls and matching bath, its piles of
matching towels, the bowl of soaps, the bath essences
and powders.

'Luxury,' said Charity and wandered back into the
bedroom. There were a couple of small easy-chairs
with lamp-tables beside them, and along the remaining
wall there were sliding doors. She opened one and saw
the vastness of the wardrobe behind them. A far cry
from her own room at home. She closed the door again
and padded over to the window. It was raining; a grey
dripping day, hardly calculated to raise her spirits.
Perhaps bed wasn't such a bad idea; she started toward
it and then halted abruptly as there was a tap on the
door and the professor walked in.

He shut the door behind him and stood leaning against it. 'Well, well. Feeling rebellious?' He studied her at his leisure and she turned her back on him, very conscious of the black eye. 'No need to do that, Charity. Yours isn't the first black eye I've seen. Get back into bed, there's a good girl.'

He spoke in his usual placid manner but she knew that he meant it. She nipped across the expanse of thick cream carpet and jumped into bed and pulled the covers up to her chin. She regretted this at once; all that rushing about had started up the ache in her face again.

'Silly girl,' said the professor. But he said it in a voice that belied the words. He drew a chair up to the bed and took her hand. 'I'll make myself quite clear. You'll stay in bed for the rest of the day, tomorrow you may get up and you will stay here, doing nothing. On the day after that you may go home.'

'When can I come back to work?'

'That is something we'll talk about in a day or two. You can hardly show that eye to my patients; they'll think I beat you and I'll lose my practice!'

She chuckled, comfortably drowsy, content to lie quiet with her hand tucked in his. Presently her eyelids closed. An hour later Aunt Emily, creeping softly in, was surprised to find them both asleep, still holding hands. She heaved a sigh of pure pleasure and crept away again. When later the professor presented himself in his sitting room to join her for tea, she greeted him with an air of pleased surprise and the remark that it was nice that he had been able to get home for tea.

Charity got up the next day after the professor had pronounced her eye to be making good progress. The swelling was subsiding and she was able to open it and peer through the narrow slit. 'You'll wear the eyeshade for another few days,' said the professor. 'Your eye had quite a blow and needs a rest. Potter around the house today—go where you like, only don't disturb anything on my desk.' He gave her an encouraging pat on the shoulder and went away. It was the professor who had said that; Jake—the Jake of their shopping and skiing—had gone. For good, probably, she told herself as she dressed.

She spent the day with Aunt Emily and the Snooks in devoted attendance. She had speculated about living in comfort—no, in luxury—and now she was experiencing it. Very nice, too, but without Jake it meant nothing at all. She ate the delicious lunch Snook set before them and then wandered round the house, admiring the portraits on its walls and running an appreciative finger along the lovely old furniture, picturing him living there with his Brenda. It was like a knife turning in a wound and did no good at all.

He didn't return until the evening, in time to join them for drinks before dinner. Charity, asked one or two tentative questions about how they were managing without her at the consulting rooms, but somehow she was fobbed off and the conversation was gently turned to general topics.

They went back to the drawing room for coffee and while Aunt Emily was pouring it the telephone rang. The professor lifted the receiver of the extension by his chair, said, 'Wyllie-Lyon here,' and listened. Beyond a grunt or two he said nothing until the speaker had finished.

'I'll come right away,' he said briefly and got up from his chair.

'I'm afraid they want me at Augustine's. I'l be leaving first thing in the morning so I'll bid you good night. There is no reason why you shouldn't go home tomorrow, Charity, but if you would like to do so, I should be delighted for you both to stay as long as you wish.'

Aunt Emily broke into speech. Of course they would go home the next day; she was anxious to take up the reins of her own household again. Besides, there was the Fancy Fair in a week's time. And they could never thank Jake sufficiently for his kindness and hospitality.

To all of which he listened with a grave courtesy before turning to Charity. 'And you will keep the shade on, Charity, and continue the treatment.'

'Yes. Oh, yes I will, but I can come back to work, can't I? The day after tomorrow? My eye is so much better . . .'

He lifted a finger and stroked her cheek gently. 'You will do as I say, my dear. There is no need to rush things, we are managing very well.'

He glanced round to where Aunt Emily was bent over her knitting. He pulled Charity through the door into the hall and closed it behind him.

'I shall miss you,' he said softly.

He put his hand on her shoulders and when she looked up at him kissed her slowly. She stared into his face, her heart hammering against her ribs so that she had no breath. All the same, the words came tumbling out before she could stop them.

'I'll miss you, too, Jake.' And, when he smiled, 'You know, don't you? You know that I love you?' She added wildly, 'I don't know why I'm telling you. I suppose because I can't keep it a secret any longer . . .'

The front door opened and Snook crossed the hall. 'I've brought your car round, sir, seeing that it was the hospital phoning.'

Jake nodded. 'Thanks, Snook. Don't wait up. I'll let myself in. I'll leave just after seven o'clock tomorrow.' He included Charity and Snook in his quiet good night as he left the house, his face quite impassive.

Charity stood mute. She would have given anything to have left unsaid the words she had just uttered. Before long she was going to feel awful about it, and there was the little matter of seeing Jake again. Presently she asked, 'How did you know that it was the hospital, Snook?'

'The calls come through to the kitchen, miss, and I switch them through to wherever the professor happens to be.'

She nodded. 'Is the professor going away again?'

'Only to Birmingham to give a lecture, miss. He will be back again late tomorrow.'

'We'll be gone.'

'I'm sorry to hear that miss. Me and Mrs Snook have enjoyed looking after you and Miss Graham.'

'Thank you, Snook.' She mustered a smile. 'I'm going to bed. I'll just say good night to my aunt.'

Aunt Emily was disposed to chat. 'Since we're going home tomorrow I think I will go directly after lunch, dear, and do some shopping. You can stay home and have a rest.'

'Of course, Aunty, but I think I'll not go rushing back with you after lunch. I've not had any exercise for a couple of days; I'll walk part of the way and get a taxi back when I'm tired. I really do need the fresh air.'

'Yes, dear, probably you are quite right, although you look very flushed.'

She proffered a cheek for Charity's kiss and picked up her knitting again.

She packed her overnight bag in the morning and

after lunch waved goodbye to her aunt and a rather puzzled Snook. She had had to explain to him about getting some fresh air and he hadn't looked entirely convinced. He would have liked her to have gone with them, or at least gone back to the professor's house after her walk and allowed him to drive her home.

She wished Mrs Snook goodbye, put on her outside things, tied a scarf on her head to cover the eye patch as much as possible, and left the house.

It was only a short walk to the consulting rooms. She opened the street door and went along to the waiting room and went inside.

Mrs Kemp's head appeared round the half open door of the consulting room. 'Charity! Hallo, dear . . .' She sounded flustered and the look of consternation on her face led Charity to say half laughing, 'Well, don't look so shattered—it's only me. I'm on my way home and I couldn't resist coming in to see the pile of work waiting for me.'

'Well,' said Mrs Kemp, 'I don't know . . .' She stood back and let Charity go past her. through the consulting room to her own office. There was someone sitting at her desk typing. A not very young woman with a friendly face. She looked up as Charity came to a surprised halt and smiled uncertainly.

'Oh, I expect the professor got a temp—he didn't say, but he told me you were managing without me. Well, I'll be back in a couple of days now.' She went right up to the desk and held out her hand. 'I'm Charity Graham.'

'Mrs Marks. How do you do. I'm sorry about your eye.'

There was a silence which Mrs Kemp broke. 'Will you have a cup of tea, Charity? The professor is away until tomorrow.' She hesitated. 'Look dear, there is no reason why you shouldn't know—I expect he has been too busy to tell you.' She gave Mrs Marks an imploring look and that lady went on, 'I'm sure he forgot and perhaps he didn't know that you would be coming here. You see, I'm to replace you.' She saw the look on Charity's face and said quickly. 'Please don't be too upset. He told me that he was making changes in the office and asked me to take over from you. Perhaps he has something else lined up for you.'

Charity said in a stiff little voice. 'Yes, perhaps he has.' The bottom had just dropped out of her world; she wanted to run to the furthermost part of the country and jump off the edge. She had gone white, but now she felt the colour flooding her face. To have told Jake that she loved him, and all the time he had known that someone else was doing her work. He must have wanted to get rid of her and the black eye had given him just the excuse he needed. Her day-dreams had turned into a nightmare. Her own silly fault for imagining even for a moment that he liked her; it had been nothing but kindness on his part. Well, she would save them both the embarrassment of meeting again. She took a steadying breath. 'Mrs Kemp, be a dear and give the professor a message from me, will you? He said something about having another look at my eye, but I'm going away for a week or two . . .'

'But you said . . . You thought you were coming back,' said Mrs Kemp.

'Oh, yes, I know,' Charity lied valiantly, 'but the professor told me not to hurry back and now there is no need anyway. I'm planning to visit some cousins in the country—I can go to their doctor.' She summoned a smile. 'I must go, My aunt's expecting me home for tea.'

She shook hands and wished them all the best in a bright voice and made a remark or two to Mrs Kemp about her two boys as she walked to the door.

She walked all the way home and Aunt Emily took one look at her and said, 'My dear Charity, what have you been doing? You look terrible.'

'I'm a little tired. If you don't mind I'll go to bed. I'll just say hallo to Father.'

Ready for bed, she remembered something she had to tell Aunt Emily. She pattered downstairs and into the kitchen, accepted the bowl of soup that lady urged upon her and said as casually as was possible, 'If the professor should come or phone, will you tell him that I've gone away? That you don't know when I'll be back.' She spooned scalding soup into a mouth which was unsteady. 'I don't want to talk about it, Aunt Emily, but I can't—simply can't—see Jake again.'

She abandoned the soup and made for the door where she turned to say in a voice which didn't sound like hers at all, 'He has sacked me—there is someone else doing my work.'

She fled before her aunt could say a word.

The three days which followed were the longest she had ever lived through. Her eye was open again but still ringed with yellow and green; there was no point in trying to get another job until she looked normal again. And the professor neither called nor telephoned. Happy to have his problems solved for him, she thought bitterly, and plunged into a welter of knitting for the Fancy Fair in two days' time. If things had been different, she thought sadly, I'd have been knitting this ridiculous woolly cap for Jake junior. She sniffed away the threat of tears, added it to the pile waiting to be priced and cast on stitches for another matinée jacket.

It was a relief that her aunt made no effort to discover what had gone wrong; indeed, she talked about everything else under the sun, never once mentioning the fact that Charity would have to look for another job fairly soon. And as for her father, beyond observing that she looked off colour, he had nothing to say.

She accompanied her aunt down to the church hall on the evening before the fair, helped her set up her stall and arrange the articles for sale upon it, helped the ladies in charge of teas to assemble their cups and saucers, and then went back home, where she ate the supper set before her and went to bed early. A mistake, for she didn't sleep, and went down to breakfast in the morning looking a pale reflection of herself.

The fair was to be opened at two o'clock. She helped her aunt around the house, ate almost no lunch and spent a long time doing her face and hair. There were purple shadows under her eyes and the tip of her nose was still fairly pink from her crying. There was no disguising the bruising round her eye; she did the best she could, got into a tweed suit and a silk blouse, found her outdoor things and went down to join her aunt.

It was a dreary day, chilly and damp and anyone forsaking their fireside for the pleasures of the Fancy Fair must be out of their minds, Charity decided, slowing her steps to keep pace with Aunt Emily. But apparently there were those who weren't too keen on their own firesides; ten minutes after they arrived at the hall, the doors were flung open and a horde of people pounded in.

'Like the January sales,' said Charity, watching two ladies fight in a well-bred manner over an embroidered bedspread. But soon she had no time to look around her; the baby garment stall always did well. After an hour she replenished its emptiness from her stocks behind the stall and had sold almost all of these when she looked up from wrapping a baby's bonnet in tissue paper to see the professor coming towards her.

Her heart stopped and then thundered on again, twice as fast. She applied herself to giving change as though her life depended on it, willing him to go away. Only he didn't. He came to a halt before her and with no customers waiting she was forced to look at him.

She said in a small high voice, 'Good afternoon, Professor. If you want to buy something I think the book stall might interest you. There is nothing here.'

He picked up a small woolly cap with a bobble on top. 'This interests me far more than books. I think our eldest would look delightful in this thing. Besides, there is something here—you. I'm deeply interested in you, my darling Charity.'

He paused with no sign of impatience while she sold a pair of mitts, taking as long as possible.

Charity felt light-headed. She had spent several days in utter misery, never quite free of Jake in her thoughts although she had struggled to forget him, and now here he was and she was ready to sink through the floor. The thought that he might not have heard her telling him that she loved him flashed through her mind, to be instantly dismissed. His hearing was excellent.

She said coolly, 'Do please go away.' And then, when he didn't budge an inch, 'You sacked me ...' She sniffed away a threat of tears. 'And if you've come here because of what I told you, you can go away again—now.'

He put out a hand and carefully removed the baby's bonnet she was screwing into a shapeless mass of knitting.

'Be sensible, darling, of course I sacked you. I do not want a wife who sits behind a desk all day pounding a typewriter. I want her at home, ordering my household, looking after the babies, dressing up to come dining and dancing, wearing beautiful clothes because she's a beautiful girl, loaded, if she wants to be, with diamonds, skimming down the mountains at Flam, learning to love my family.' He smiled down at her and she studied every line of his face. 'It will be wonderful to come home to you,' he said.

'Brenda . . .' asked Charity and tried not to sound too eager to know.

'Like your Sidney, something that became a habit without realising it.'

He glanced round at the crowded hall. 'Is there somewhere quiet . . .?' And, when she hesitated, 'I'll come round to your side.'

'Jake, no, you simply can't.' She stopped there because he could and he would if he wanted to. 'Perhaps Aunt Emily . . .'

That lady had been watching them avidly. Now, in answer to a look from the professor, she nipped down to Charity's end, ignoring a stout lady waving a toddler's playsuit at her.

'Miss Graham, I want a few minutes with Charity— somewhere quiet. Could you possibly manage?'

She beamed at them both. 'Of course. The pantry— second door on the left.'

She trotted back and allowed the stout lady to have her purchase cheap out of sheer happiness.

The pantry was a long narrow room with a sink

down one wall and tea urns down the other. The professor closed the door behind them and looked around him.

'Not perhaps the most romantic of surroundings.' He put his hands on Charity's shoulders and twisted her round to face him. 'I've been in love with you since the very first moment I set eyes on you. You were standing on a chair in Miss Hudson's office changing a light bulb. I took one look and knew that there would never be anyone else but you.'

Charity heaved a great sigh. 'I didn't know then, but it's been you all the time. And I did try to be a model secretary.'

He folded her in his arms. 'You were, my darling, most efficient. Will you marry me, my dearest? Have I told you that I love you above everything in the world?'

'No, but you have now,' said Charity, 'and yes, I will marry you, dear Jake.'

She had no chance to say more; she was being kissed in a manner which left her in no doubt as to Jake's feelings. And when the door opened and two ladies, bent on making tea, came in, he paused only long enough to glance at them and wish them a polite good afternoon.

They stood in the open doorway, gazing their fill. Never mind the tea urns boiling away, this was romance, and in a most unlikely place. That nice little Miss Graham too. They went out again and closed the door soundlessly behind them.

Charity, who hadn't even heard or seen them, wreathed her arms round Jake's neck. When she had the opportunity she said, 'We have a great deal to talk about, Jake.'

'Indeed yes, my little love, but let us get married first.'

Which seemed a good idea. There was no need to speak, so she kissed him instead.

Six exciting series for you every month... from Harlequin

Harlequin Romance·
The series that started it all

Tender, captivating and heartwarming...
love stories that sweep you off to faraway places
and delight you with the magic of love.

◆

Harlequin Presents·
Powerful contemporary love stories...as individual as the women who read them

The No. 1 romance series...
exciting love stories for you, the woman of today...
a rare blend of passion and dramatic realism.

◆

Harlequin Superromance®
It's more than romance... it's Harlequin Superromance

A sophisticated, contemporary romance-fiction
series, providing you with a longer,
more involving read...a richer mix of complex plots,
realism and adventure.

Harlequin American Romance
Harlequin celebrates the American woman...

...by offering you romance stories written about American women, by American women for American women. This series offers you contemporary romances uniquely North American in flavor and appeal.

◆

Harlequin Temptation
Passionate stories for today's woman

An exciting series of sensual, mature stories of love...dilemmas, choices, resolutions... all contemporary issues dealt with in a true-to-life fashion by some of your favorite authors.

◆

Harlequin Intrigue
Because romance can be quite an adventure

Harlequin Intrigue, an innovative series that blends the romance you expect... with the unexpected. Each story has an added element of intrigue that provides a new twist to the Harlequin tradition of romance excellence.

Harlequin Books

PROD-A-2

What the press says about Harlequin romance fiction...

"When it comes to romantic novels...
Harlequin is the indisputable king."
— *New York Times*

"...always with an upbeat, happy ending."
— *San Francisco Chronicle*

"Women have come to trust these
stories about contemporary people,
set in exciting foreign places."
— *Best Sellers*, New York

"The most popular reading matter of
American women today."
— *Detroit News*

"...a work of art."
— *Globe & Mail*, Toronto

What readers say about Harlequin romance fiction...

"I absolutely adore Harlequin romances! They are fun and relaxing to read, and each book provides a wonderful escape."
—N.E.,* Pacific Palisades, California

"Harlequin is the best in romantic reading."
—K.G.,* Philadelphia, Pennsylvania

"Harlequins have been my passport to the world. I have been many places without ever leaving my doorstep."
—P.Z.,* Belvedere, Illinois

"My praise for the warmth and adventure your books bring into my life."
—D.F.,* Hicksville, New York

"A pleasant way to relax after a busy day."
—P.W.,* Rector, Arkansas

*Names available on request.

ATTRACTIVE, SPACE SAVING BOOK RACK

Display your most prized novels on this handsome and sturdy book rack. The hand-rubbed walnut finish will blend into your library decor with quiet elegance, providing a practical organizer for your favorite hard-or soft-covered books.

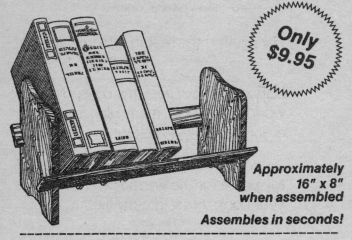

Only $9.95

Approximately 16" x 8" when assembled

Assembles in seconds!

To order, rush your name, address and zip code, along with a check or money order for $10.70* ($9.95 plus 75¢ postage and handling) payable to *Harlequin Reader Service*:

Harlequin Reader Service
Book Rack Offer
901 Fuhrmann Blvd.
P.O. Box 1325
Buffalo, NY 14269-1325

Offer not available in Canada.

BKR-1R

*New York residents add appropriate sales tax.